Cole threw a leg over the big machine and held out his hand.

"Hop on," he said with a lopsided grin that made her mind go momentarily blank.

She swallowed hard, reminded herself this was just a ride home—on a motorcycle—and took his hand. Climbing on behind him, she sat stiffly.

"How long are you in town for your visit?" she asked, then wanted to kick herself. She hoped he was leaving the next day. He was *not* her forever cowboy!

The engine burst to life. He glanced over his shoulder at her and his eyes glinted in the moonlight. "Depends on a few things, but I'm here for a few weeks."

A few weeks. "That long?" she said, but her words were drowned out by the roar of the motorcycle. Or so she thought until Cole shot her another sly look.

"Yeah," he said, over the growl of the motorcycle. "I think it's going to be real interesting. Now hang on."

Oh, dear…

Books by Debra Clopton

Love Inspired

*The Trouble with
  Lacy Brown
*And Baby Makes Five
*No Place Like Home
*Dream a Little Dream
*Meeting Her Match
*Operation: Married
  by Christmas
*Next Door Daddy

*Her Baby Dreams
*The Cowboy Takes a Bride
*Texas Ranger Dad
*Small-Town Brides
"A Mule Hollow Match"
*His Cowgirl Bride
**Her Forever Cowboy

*Mule Hollow
**Men of Mule Hollow

DEBRA CLOPTON

was a 2004 Golden Heart finalist in the inspirational category, a 2006 Inspirational Readers' Choice Award winner, a 2007 Golden Quill award winner and a finalist for the 2007 American Christian Fiction Writers Book of the Year Award. She praises the Lord each time someone votes for one of her books, and takes it as an affirmation that she is exactly where God wants her to be.

Debra is a hopeless romantic and loves to create stories with lively heroines and the strong heroes who fall in love with them. But most importantly she loves showing her characters living their faith, seeking God's will in their lives one day at a time. Her goal is to give her readers an entertaining story that will make them smile, hopefully laugh and always feel God's goodness as they read her books. She has found the perfect home for her stories writing for the Love Inspired line and still has to pinch herself just to see if she really is awake and living her dream.

When she isn't writing, she enjoys taking road trips, reading and spending time with her two sons, Chase and Kris. She loves hearing from readers and can be reached through her Web site, www.debraclopton.com, or by mail at P.O. Box 1125, Madisonville, Texas 77864.

Her Forever Cowboy
Debra Clopton

Steeple
Hill®

Published by Steeple Hill Books™

STEEPLE HILL BOOKS

Steeple
Hill®

Recycling programs
for this product may
not exist in your area.

ISBN-13: 978-0-373-81451-0

HER FOREVER COWBOY

www.SteepleHill.com

Printed in U.S.A.

When my spirit grows faint within me, it is you,
O Lord, who know my way.
—*Psalms* 142:3

This book is dedicated with much love and appreciation to my new friends
Sharon Howell and Jo Anne Faerber.
Jo Anne, I'm so glad you came to my book signing and brought Sharon to meet me. God blessed me that day—you gals have inspired me to step out of my comfort zone this year and let God lead me forward. Bless you both for listening to His voice!

Chapter One

Susan Worth rubbed her eyes, fighting the exhaustion threatening to overtake her. She'd spent most of the night saving the life of an unborn calf and mother and her adrenaline had kept her moving. Emergency calls had kept her out three nights in a row and she was dead on her feet—the drone of her truck's engine and the dark, deserted road were working against her. Tightening her fingers around the steering wheel, she dug deep, sat up straight and concentrated on keeping her eyes open.

She still had an hour's drive to make it home. Once again she was alone in the middle of the night on a deserted road, halfway along the seventy-mile stretch between the tiny ranching town of Mule

Hollow and the larger town of Ranger, where her clinic and apartment were—for the time being.

She loved her job and had worked hard to have her career as a small-town vet. But the exhausting pace was sometimes too much to take. The threat of falling asleep at the wheel was a risk for anyone who covered a full day's schedule and handled all emergency calls. More so for her, since her large-animal business had grown so big over in the Mule Hollow area—great for the bottom line, but bad on the body.

And bad on her personal life. With her hours growing longer and longer, quality life after work had become almost nonexistent.

She blinked hard and glanced at the clock—2:00 a.m. This was the third night in a row she'd been out this late. Third day in a row she'd not had time to catch up on lost sleep. Daytime emergencies and scheduled small-animal appointments had her hands tied, but she'd been warned it would be this way. The retiring older vet, a male, had told her that since she was a woman she should concentrate on small animals and leave the big stuff to a man. That advice hadn't sat well with her.

She smiled, tiredly remembering how insulted she'd been. But her dad always said, "Susan, take advice, then do it your way." And that was what she'd done.

She'd bought her clinic and embraced the loyal, small-animal clientele that came with it. But though she dearly loved and adored dogs and cats, her passion was working with large stock. She'd gone after that clientele with a vengeance and proved to the men who'd give her a chance that she knew what she was doing. She loved horses and cattle and as her reputation grew, so had the business. Now she was burning the candle at both ends and in between, too.

She loved her life. She really did…but something had to give, and she understood this clearly. Either that or she was going to crash and burn. *Maybe right now if you don't snap to!*

She rubbed her neck and watched the road. A few weeks ago she'd finally forced herself to come to the conclusion that she wanted a change…a family. She'd lost her mother during childbirth and had been raised by her dad. Since his death she'd felt so alone, and no amount of work could fix that. Her dad had filled his life with work and she'd striven all her life to please him, but she needed more. He'd had her…she had no one now.

As if God was giving her the nod, she'd gotten an offer for her small-animal clinic almost the instant she'd come to the realization that she wanted to make a change. God's timing—what an amazing thing.

Sighing, she shook her head to wake herself up—this week was proving to her that she'd made the right decision. She hoped relocating her large-animal clinic to Mule Hollow, to the heart of her business, would give the heart of her love life a boost, too. Only time would tell.

Susan shook her head, her chin dipped and she realized she'd closed her eyes momentarily. She still had fifty miles to go.

Focus, Susan. She took a deep breath and pressed the button to roll down her window. She inhaled the fresh air. She thought about hanging her head out the window, but didn't. Instead she let her thoughts churn. It wasn't that she couldn't find a date. She managed short relationships from time to time. Short being the keynote, because either the guys ended up being big losers or the ones who were nice were interested in a woman who wasn't so focused on her work. As most of them put it, "a woman who isn't owned by her work." Who could blame them? Really, a man wanted a woman to be there for him. A woman who worked a hundred or more hours, on a normal week, wasn't exactly what a man would consider marriage material....

Susan's eyes closed.

A flash of light had her jerking awake to see a motorcycle in the beam of her head-lights just as her truck swerved off the road. And straight for a stand of trees!

"Oh, my goodness!" she exclaimed as the truck bounded over the rough ground and the back end fishtailed and swerved around. Susan fought for control as the truck slid broadside toward the large solid trees—but it was useless. One thought hit her as she held on tight and everything started to spin—she'd made the decision to change up her life, but maybe she'd made the call a little too late.

The driver was a woman.

Her arms were crossed over the top of the steering wheel and her forehead was resting on them. She wasn't moving.

Cole Turner's heart thundered against his

ribs. Playing chicken on his Harley at two in the morning with an oversize hunk of truck hadn't been his idea of a great welcome home.

But it was exactly what had just happened.

His motorcycle helmet fell unheeded to the ground as he placed a hand on the open window. "Ma'am. Are you okay?" His gut tightened with tension when she didn't answer and the hair on the back of his neck stood up. "Ma'am," he asked again, with more force. His adrenaline kicked into high gear and he spoke louder. "Can you hear me?" When she still didn't respond, he reached through the open window to check for a pulse. Her skin was warm, but at his touch she lifted her head. Relief washed through him as she eyed him groggily.

Susan Worth.

He recognized her—she was the vet his brother Seth used at their ranch in Mule Hollow. Seth seemed overly impressed by her and often sang her praises when they talked on the phone.

But Cole hadn't been nearly so impressed when Seth had introduced them at his wedding six months ago—the woman hadn't given Cole the time of day.

"Cole—" she said, her voice wobbling.

The wobble got him, and despite her snub before, he felt for her. "Cole Turner, at your service," he drawled, tugging open her door and offering her a grin and a hand. Getting her out of the truck would help put some color back into her face. She was as pale as the shimmery moonlight cascading over her. "Are you okay?"

"I fell asleep…" she said, her stunned eyes holding his. "I can't believe I fell asleep." Disbelief turned to disgust.

Scowling, she slid from the seat, ignoring his offered hand. He reached to help her anyway. All long-legged and lanky in her jeans and boots, she was almost as tall as he was. He'd forgotten how beautiful she was, even with weariness and anger etching her face.

"Well, you've been working hard," he said, trying to make her feel better. He was assuming her being out this late was work-related, since she was a vet.

"No excuse," she snapped. "I shouldn't have fallen asleep."

So the doc wasn't going to give herself a break. "You're right, you shouldn't have. But you did." That got him a startled glare. "Fact is, you look like you're about to drop on your feet. That bein' the case, what are you doin' out here in the middle of nowhere at *two* in the morning when you are so worn out?" And what was he doing sticking his nose where it didn't belong?

"I am a *vet*. I was heading home to Ranger after running an emergency call—for your brother, actually. We almost lost a momma and her unborn calf."

"You were at *our* place? Seth let you head back to Ranger in this condition?" Cole's temper shot sky-high. Bone weariness hung over her like a cloak—Seth had to have seen that. "What was my brother thinking? One glance at you and anyone can see you're in no shape to travel. Look in the mirror—you look like you haven't slept in days."

Her shoulders squared. "I beg your pardon. Seth didn't *let* me do anything. I did my job, saved that calf, then left—it wasn't any of Seth's business what I did after that. And it sure isn't your business—"

That did it. "Lady, it's two stinkin' a.m. When you almost ran me down with your truck it sorta *made* it my business. So don't even think about getting defensive. Four seconds farther along the road and you'd have been topping that hill the same time I was. You'd have wiped me out with your big truck while you were taking your little nap."

He was stepping across boundaries and he knew it. But he'd been involved in far too many rescues and recoveries that had nothing to do with careless acts on the part of the victims…good people died from no fault of their own every day. *This* was carelessness on the doc's part and he'd witnessed it—that made it his business. Whether she wanted it to be or not.

He hadn't asked for it, but he wasn't the kind to back off from what was right if it would save a life. Even that of a gal who'd taken one look at him six months ago and stuck her pretty nose so high in the air that if it had started to rain she'd have drowned on the spot.

Nope, if there was one thing he had no use for, it was a stuck-up woman. But he couldn't, in all good conscience, just walk off, either.

Being nearly run down by Susan was the last thing he'd expected when his brother Wyatt had basically blackmailed him into coming home for a visit. It would have suited him fine not to have seen her again while he was in town.

Susan suddenly lifted fingers to her temple and, looking at her, he thought his words might have hit home.

"If you must know I've had emergency runs three nights in a row," she said. "Plus I've had packed schedules during the day, so that doesn't leave much time to sleep."

Her excuse slid off Cole like water off a duck's back. "Some things you make time for. A dead vet doesn't keep appointments—no matter how important they may seem. Do you not realize what a narrow escape you just had?"

She flinched. "It didn't happen, though—"

"*Hardheaded woman!*" Cole shook his head, realizing this was going nowhere. "This is a waste of time. Come on, I'll take you home. We'll worry about your truck in the morning."

Susan felt as if she was in a big tunnel full of thick fog as she stared at Cole. She was still trying to process everything that had just happened. Falling asleep at the wheel was horrible; nearly running over a motorcycle rider was horrific; nearly killing herself was terrible. But looking up after all of it to find drop-dead gorgeous, fly-by-the-seat-of-his-pants Cole Turner leaning in her window was her payback for all of it. *She'd almost run the poor man down!*

She could only stare at him as he jumped all over her. His T-shirt-clad chest was bowed out and his eyes were clashing with hers, and like the cold waves of an angry ocean he took her breath away. It had been the same way at his brother's wedding when she'd first met him.

"Well," he drawled, lifting a ridiculously attractive eyebrow—*oh, for cryin' out loud!* She was so tired she was now noticing how attractive his eyebrows were.

"Look, I'm sorry," she said, struggling to get her head back on straight. "I'm doing the best I can at the moment."

"It's not good enough."

"Excuse me." She might feel guilty, but if he thought he was going to stand there making her feel worse with all his high-handed tactics he was wrong—matter of fact, he was starting to irritate her. "I'm not going anywhere with you. My truck is fine—"

"You're not fine."

"I am, too," she argued. "So what are *you* doing out here at two in the morning? I thought you were rescuing people on the coast."

"I decided it was time to come home for a visit. Somewhere around Waco, I decided to drive on through the night. Good thing, too, since you were the one in need of being rescued…which sort of puts a spin on you being fine." He cocked his head to the side, sending a thick lock of hair sliding forward across his forehead.

Susan rubbed her temple and stared at the man Mule Hollow folks called the rolling stone. He'd left town straight out of high school and rarely came home to visit. He was probably wishing he'd stayed away tonight.

She knew she sounded ridiculous every time she denied being worn-out. The look in his eyes told her he knew that if he blew hard enough she'd topple over.

"You're right," she said reluctantly. "I did need your help. But now I'm fine. Really. I almost ran you over. The last thing I'm going to do is make you take me the hour back to Ranger." Especially on a motorcycle…she was terrified of the things. Not that she'd dare tell him that, she thought as she turned back to her truck.

"Whoa, there. Look at it from my point of

view." He placed a hand on her arm to halt her. "I can't let you get back in that truck. What kind of man would I be to do that?"

His hand was warm and the pads of his fingers were rough against her skin—a tingle of awareness waltzed slowly through her. Whoa—the man was trying to take charge of her business and she was thinking about tingling skin! What was wrong with her? This would not do. "Cole, I don't need you—I can take care of myself," she said, locking firm eyes on him. She'd spent her life learning to stand on her own two feet. She didn't need a virtual stranger telling her what to do. The last thing she expected was for him to reach past her and snag her keys from the ignition.

"Obviously there's no reasoning with you," Cole said. "I hate to break it to you, but you're comin' with me. End of story."

"Cole Turner, give me those keys!" she exclaimed. "Right this minute."

"I like that fire you got goin' on there, darlin'. But no can do. See, a friend wouldn't let a friend drink and drive, and I won't let you sleep and drive."

Glowering at him in the moonlight, she plopped one hand palm out. "Then I'll sleep in my truck. Hand over my keys. Now."

"Not happening." He proceeded to step around her, blocking her from the inside of the truck as he slipped the key back in the ignition, pressed the automatic button and waited as the window rolled closed.

"Cole Turner," Susan gritted out from behind him.

His back burned from the heat of her wrath. Ignoring it, he slipped the key safely into his pocket, locked the truck door then slammed it firmly shut. When he turned around she had her hands on her hips shooting daggers at him with those amazing electric-blue eyes. He did like her eyes.

"You are not funny, Cole. I want my keys."

She was tenacious. "You might as well give it up, Doc. I'm more stubborn than you, and you're going for a ride with me and that's it." Snagging his helmet from the ground, he strode up the embankment toward his ride. "Come on, Doc," he called over his shoulder. "We're burning up precious darkness standing here arguing. There is nothing more you can do."

A loud huff said what she thought of him.

No surprise there…he wasn't exactly impressed with her, either. Still, her footsteps, make that stomps, behind him brought a smile to his lips.

Chapter Two

Maybe sleep would help.

Everything was sort of mingled and mixed in a confusing way in her fuddled brain. It was hard to separate them. She was definitely going to need a few hours of sleep to ensure she didn't make some crazy mistake—like making goo-goo eyes at the man. *So* not happening.

Of course him acting all me-man-you-woman on her was helping toss some cold ice on the situation. Taking her keys like he did—out of concern or whatever—didn't sit well. She was embarrassed beyond belief that she'd nearly run him down. She was reacting badly—in part because of the fact that she found the man unnervingly attractive. Cole was tall at about six-three, which for a gal of five foot ten inches, like her, made for a nice combination. He was lanky lean, with an athletic grace about him. She had a feeling he was a jogger…but she wasn't about to ask him.

"Put this on," Cole demanded, swinging around so quickly she practically ran him over. He steadied her with his hand then held his helmet out to her.

"What about you?" she asked, holding the slick red helmet away from her.

He took it back and settled it on her head. "You wear the helmet." He stared hard at her as he pushed her hair out of her face and, oddly, his actions touched her.

Totally out of her comfort zone, she stood like a deer in headlights as he tugged the strap snug. She fought to seem calm.

"It's a bit large, but better than nothing," he continued, thankfully not picking up on the battle that was waging in her head. "Not that I plan on letting anything happen to you."

His gentle words caused a rush of butterflies to settle in her stomach. Not good at all. Cole Turner was a restless spirit. A wandering man.

She backed away from his touch, feeling

foolish, especially when his own expression said nothing at all about returning her infatuation.

Oh, no, instead he threw a leg over the big machine, glanced over his shoulder and gave her a lopsided grin. "Hop on."

She swallowed hard, reminded herself this was her only option for getting home then climbed on behind him. She sat stiffly, really not wanting to stretch her arms around his waist.

"How, um, long are you in town for your visit?" she asked, needing something to fill the moment. She hoped he was leaving the next day.

Instead of answering, he cranked up the bike and the engine burst to life. He glanced her way and his eyes glinted in the moonlight. "Depends on a few things, but I might be here for a few weeks."

A few weeks! "That long?" she squeaked the words out. Thankfully they were drowned out by the roar of the motorcycle.

Or so she thought.

"Yeah," Cole said with a grin. "That long. Now hang on. It's time to get you home so you can get some rest."

Like that's going to happen. She was

wide-awake; her arms were wrapped around Cole Turner—the handsome nomad.

The rolling stone. From what she knew of him he would never be happy unless he was roaming the country. She'd never be satisfied until she was settled and had a family, so this infatuation was ridiculous. Sleep. She needed it! If she wasn't so tired she wouldn't be engaging in this weird assortment of thoughts.

A very long time ago she hadn't thought she wanted a family, either, but…things changed. She sighed and tried again to quiet her mind.

"You okay back there?" Cole called over his shoulder a few miles down the road. His words were almost lost in the night as the air rushed over them. She gave up and settled closer to him, nodding her helmeted head against his shoulder. Weariness sank over her as they rode and thankfully overcame most of her wayward thoughts.

He didn't try to talk to her over the drone of the engine, blessedly. He made sure she hadn't fallen asleep every once in a while but other than that he left her alone. She had to admit that he might have been right about her not having any business driving herself.

"That's it," she said almost an hour later when her clinic's small lighted sign came into view on the outskirts of Ranger. "My apartment is out back." She pointed out the drive around the far side of the metal building and then past the holding pens.

"You live back here by yourself?"

The censure in his voice was unmistakable and it sent her an immediate reality check. "It's small, but it worked for me," she said when the little apartment that had been built onto the back of the barn area came into view. She didn't tell him that soon it would no longer be her home.

"No one has ever tried to bother you back here?" He turned the engine off.

Susan wasted no time getting off the machine and removing the helmet—she didn't plan on giving him the chance to do it for her. "No, they haven't," she said, holding out her hand. "Thanks for everything. Now may I have my keys."

He got off the bike and dug her keys out of his pocket. But instead of handing the keys to her he began taking her truck key from the ring. "What are you doing?"

"I'm taking this. As soon as it's daylight— in about three hours—I'll crawl up under it and make sure you didn't tear anything up while you were plowing up turf. If everything checks out, I'll have your truck here by seven or eight. You won't be doing calls before then I hope."

She didn't like him taking control like this. But since she could tell there was no sense arguing, she didn't. She was too tired. She took the rest of the keys from him. "Eight will be fine. Thank you," she managed, though her jaw ached from clenching it.

He smiled and she could practically hear him thinking "checkmate."

Maybe not, though, she thought a few minutes later as she closed the door to her apartment and listened to the motorcycle purr its way back toward the pavement. The man was used to sweeping into emergency situations and taking charge. That was what he did for a living—helped in rescues, then remodeled and rebuilt after hurricanes and other disasters. So maybe there wasn't anything personal about how he was treating her.

Maybe. But as she took a quick shower and then fell into her bed—basically passing out from exhaustion—she knew she wasn't buying that notion by a long shot. Cole had pretty much made it clear that he thought she was an irresponsible fool for letting herself get so tired. He'd been doing his civic duty by keeping "the fool woman" off the streets—that was *pretty* personal. Of course, nearly running him down was, too.

"I'm just sayin' it's a fine thang you came along when ya did last night," Applegate Thornton said, his voice booming in the early morning quiet.

Cole had just crawled out from under the truck when the older man and his buddy, Stanley Orr, pulled up in their trucks, one behind the other. They'd wasted no time trotting down the incline to see what was going on with the lame truck. It shouldn't have been a surprise to see the two old friends out and about so early, since they always met at Sam's diner for coffee at sunup then played checkers all morning. Today they'd be late; Susan's mishap was of more interest to them than today's checkers game.

The seventysomething older men had been great friends of his grandfather and Cole always enjoyed seeing them on his quick trips through town. Now, he wiped his hands on his work rag and nodded. "Yes, sir," he said. "I'm not disagreeing with you. I'm glad

I was out here when I was or else Susan would still have been sitting here when you fellas drove up this morning.

"What I'm wondering is what in the world everyone is thinking when they call that woman out on the road at all hours of the night? There are other vets to call, you know." He planned to let everyone know he was unhappy about that situation and there was no better place to start than with these two. Talk about a grapevine. It didn't get any quicker than them when it came to spreading information.

Instead of answering him they looked at each other and raised their bushy brows. "Am I missing something here?" Cole asked. "You can bet I'm having a talk with my brother when I get back to the house." Oh, yeah, Seth was about to get a royal chewing out for letting Susan leave the ranch when clearly she was ready to drop. He'd told Cole once that she needed help, so why didn't she have it?

Stanley, affable, slightly plump and balding looked perplexed. "You ain't been around Susan much, have ya?"

Applegate, taller and thin as a fence post, wore his signature frown as he grunted. *"Obviously."*

Both men wore hearing aids and still their words cracked like thunder, even App's grunt stirred up the cattle milling in the pastures behind the barbed wire.

"So what does that mean?" Cole asked.

Applegate grunted again. "It means that Susan does what she wants. That gal is all-fired determined to be accepted on a man's terms. If any of us was ta tell her she ought'n ta be out that late—or *worse*, if we had livestock that needed tending and we didn't call her—" He whistled long and slow, while wagging his head.

"That's right," Stanley continued. "She'd let us have it with both barrels."

"After what I saw last night, I can believe that."

"Yup, I'm shor you did. That little gal kin be real hard-nosed when it comes to her job," Applegate said. "She don't take kindly ta bein' treated like a lady. And she's real good at what she does."

"Ain't that the truth," Stanley said.

She'd made it clear last night that she hadn't liked him taking charge. "Maybe so," he said, at last. "But I don't like it. It doesn't feel right. And it sure doesn't feel safe."

App tugged on his hat brim as the sun

shifted a bit higher over the horizon. "It'll be a little easier when she gets her office relocated here in town."

That got Cole's attention. "What do you mean?"

Stanley and Applegate grinned at each other then gave him the we-know-something-you-don't-know look. Cole knew they were also speculating at his interest in Susan. But he couldn't help that. He leaned against the truck and crossed his arms waiting for them to elaborate. He was going to have to get on the road in a few minutes but he wanted the lowdown on this.

"So…" Applegate took his time, rubbed his narrow jaw. "She didn't tell you she's bought a place on the west side of town about four miles out."

"It was two in the morning when I came across her. We weren't engaging in conversation beyond me telling her I was taking her home—" No sense elaborating on the tone of that conversation.

"Guess that went over like a basket of mad cats." Stanley chuckled. "You don't 'tell' our Susan anythang where her business is concerned. That's what we been tryin' ta tell ya."

He shouldn't have let it slip that he'd

"told" her he was taking her home. No one needed to know he'd had to hijack her keys to get her to cooperate. *Hardheaded woman.*

"So where is this place?" he asked.

"It's a small property—little house and a large metal building." Applegate was more than happy to fill him in. "It used to be that oil supply company. You remember the place? Back b'fore the oil boom busted in the eighties. B'fore ever'body moved off."

Cole nodded. "I remember." It was the beginning of the town's slow death.

"She's got some contractor comin' outta Ranger in a couple of days ta start turnin' it into her new office."

"You don't say." She was moving to Mule Hollow and hadn't mentioned it. "Is she going to live here?" he asked to clarify his assumption.

"Yup," Stanley said. "In the house on the property. I even thank she done put some stuff in thar."

When he'd made that comment about where she lived now, she'd had the opportunity to tell him and hadn't. She kept her business close to the cuff. Or she knew he'd soon find out and this was her way of telling him to mind his own business. He smiled at that. She had spunk. He pushed away from the truck.

"Well, thanks for the info, fellas. Now I better get this to her so she'll have wheels when she needs them. Wouldn't want to make her mad." That got him some slaps on the back and hoots of agreement.

Earlier, after taking her home, he'd driven the hour and a half back to the ranch and hadn't been able to stop thinking about their encounter.

He didn't stay at the ranch house when home, but down at the old stagecoach house that was the original homestead on their ranch. He always enjoyed the old house and had felt that same ole tug of nostalgia as he'd driven down the dirt road toward it. The moon had highlighted the rocky road as it wound across the pastures and as it always had, he couldn't help thinking about the others who'd traveled this same road over a hundred years ago. Men such as Doc Holliday and outlaw Sam Bass had passed by either on horseback or by stage. As a kid he'd thought it was cool and that hadn't changed as he'd aged. His great-great-great-great-grandpa Oakley had won the place in a poker game more than a century ago.

Now Applegate looked from him to his truck. "We kin follow you ta Susan's and brang you back if ya need us to."

Cole shook his head and packed up his last few things. "Thanks, but no need. I've got it covered." He figured if Susan wasn't making any calls out this direction, he'd have Seth drive to Ranger and pick him up.

After only a bit of cajoling, the tires found grip and he drove out of the ditch. App and Stanley waved him on as he headed toward Ranger—looking in his rearview, he saw them hop in their trucks and head toward town. They were driving at a fast clip; no doubt about it, everyone was about to know about last night….

Susan didn't like to show weakness, it was obvious. Was that what was driving her crazy attitude last night?

Not that he thought some determination in a woman wasn't a good thing. Before he could pull back, his thoughts went to Lori. She'd been full of determination, too; if it hadn't been for that grit she wouldn't have made it as long as she had… Six years and he still couldn't think about that sweet girl without his gut twisting up like a bull had stomped him. And just like he always did, he shoved the thoughts of her back into the dark shadows and forced all the trapped emotions down with them.

He focused instead on Susan Worth.

The woman had been careless last night and almost killed herself. It bothered him that she was so obsessed with her job that she'd take her life for granted…when others fought so hard for one more breath.

Stop it. It usually took at least a couple of weeks in one spot before restless memories drove him to move on. He'd been home less than five hours and already he was fighting with the past. Home was always the worst. It was easier to pretend things like home and hearth didn't matter when you didn't have them staring you in the face.

Wyatt better show up soon or Cole was out of here. His brothers knew he'd fallen in love with a terminally ill barrel racer.

But they'd never met Lori. She'd been more ill than he'd realized when he first met her and that had prevented any travel. She had tried hard not to fall for him—to prevent the hurt something like that could cause. She'd tried hard to ignore what he'd known from the moment he'd laid eyes on her sweet face…love didn't have a perfect timetable. It

happened even while a person was dying…
love was brutal that way. And special.

As long as he was on the road, working to
help folks, he did all right and actually
enjoyed his life. When the restless memories
threatened, he finished up what he was doing
and headed out to find a new job—a new
project.

And the recent turn of bad luck on the Gulf
of Mexico had given him plenty of choices.
Helping rebuild something a hurricane or a
tornado had taken away from a family gave
him a good feeling. It also helped the anger
at God that plagued him…he tried not to
dwell on it, and he wasn't going to now.
Only, coming back to Mule Hollow was
coming home…the place he'd longed to
bring Lori. Home reminded him too much of
how bad God's timing was and how He
seemed to pick and choose who He deemed
good enough to get a miracle. Or who didn't.

Who got their prayers answered…and
who didn't.

Home was where you brought the one you
loved…unless you weren't one of the special
ones who God shined His light on and
listened to.

Chapter Three

Susan was standing out front with a tiny, blue-haired woman and a large dog that resembled a chocolate Lab but was shaped more like a big, brown, chocolate kiss…or a gigantic tick.

Susan was far more attention-worthy than the dog, with the morning sun glinting off her corn-silk hair. But even her beautiful hair didn't compare to the smile on her face—that smile startled him so bad he ran over a curb while pulling into the parking lot.

Yup, he was the one who needed rest now. It would help him get his head back on straight—a few hours of shut-eye had sure helped the prickly vet. No doubt about that…no doubt at all.

It wasn't just the softening of the dark

circles, but she was smiling—he hadn't even got a hint of one of those last night. Though he didn't figure that was totally due to lack of sleep.

"Good morning." He got out of the truck and moved toward the women, who had been staring at him ever since he'd jumped the curb.

Susan crossed her arms and nodded—the smile gone in a flash.

But the little old lady had one big enough for the both of them. "Well, one thing's the truth, my mornin' just got better thanks to you, young man." She gave him the once-over. "My goodness, but you are a handsome fellow. Just in the nick of time, too. Bein' timely is important. Don't you think?"

"Yes, ma'am, real important—"

"Good. Good." She broke him off with a wave of her cane. "I like you—I like this one, Susan." She shot Susan a sharp eye then gave him a soft smile. "Would you mind terribly, helping Catherine Elizabeth into her car seat? Arthur, the scamp, is acting up today—been giving me and my Catherine Elizabeth both a run for our money. But *you*—" she smiled up at him, her cloudy blue eyes shining as she grabbed hold of his bicep and squeezed like she might check the ripeness of a grapefruit "—you look like you're in plenty good shape, so the old bully won't bother you. No *sirree,* he won't."

Cole looked around for Arthur with every intention of setting the so-called bully straight. He wouldn't stand by and let a man mistreat the little lady. But there wasn't anyone else around. He glanced at Susan for some kind of hint and saw that she was biting back a smile. And amazing enough her eyes were twinkling—he lost his train of thought.

"Mrs. Abernathy, may I introduce Cole Turner," she said rather loudly. "He's the one who came to my rescue last night. Cole, this is Mrs. Abernathy and *this* is the one and only Catherine Elizabeth."

Mrs. Abernathy was still holding on to his bicep with her tiny hand and gazing up at him sweetly. Catherine Elizabeth had managed to lift to her feet and lumbered over to him. She sank onto his boot like a melting blob of ice cream.

"Glad to make your acquaintance, ma'am," Cole said. "And Catherine Elizabeth, too." He glanced around again for Arthur but no man had come out of the building. They all were looking at him expectantly—waiting.

"Oh, sorry, you want me to load the dog into the car?"

"Thank you. She's just too much for me. But not you." She rubbed his arm. "You remind me of my Herman—God rest his soul. He was tall and strong, too. I'm glad Susan's found a young man like you."

"Mrs. Abernathy," Susan interjected, "he's not my, um, young man."

Mrs. Abernathy patted his arm. "Well, he should be, dear. You need a strong man, since you're such a darling, strong woman yourself. I, too, was a strong woman."

It was Cole's turn to bite back a smile. The woman wasn't even five foot and probably had never weighed a hundred pounds soaking wet in her entire life.

She gave him a knowing look. "There's more to being strong than size, young man. Arthur's just beat me down a bit through the years and I have to admit it weighs on me… makes even my strong spirit weak at times."

Cole shot Susan an inquiring glance. "Who is that?" he mouthed over the little lady's head.

"Ohh," Susan gasped. "Sorry. Mrs. A., as we affectionately call her, and Catherine Elizabeth both suffer from Arthur-itis."

Mrs. A. shook her head. "He's a mean one,

that Arthur. But the good Lord puts such nice men in my path to help out in times such as these." She let go of his arm and, leaning on her cane, she walked carefully to her car.

Watching her slow progress, Cole agreed that Arthur was a real bummer. "Will it hurt when I pick her up?" he asked Susan, staring down at the dog.

"Just be careful and she'll be okay. But don't throw your back out or anything." The last part was soft so that Mrs. Abernathy couldn't hear.

He almost laughed as he leaned down for the dog. Who did she think he was? Some kind of wimp?

"I mean it—lift from the knees," Susan said, bending over to whisper the words close to his ear.

The warmth of her breath tickled his skin and sent a shiver of awareness rippling over him. He chuckled, both from the humor in the warning and the shock of her warm breath on his skin, then he lifted—*whhoa!* The dog was deadweight.

Susan slapped him on the back. "Told you lift with the knees."

"No kiddin'." Sending her a good-natured scowl, he then gave it a fortified effort. It felt as if he was hauling a bag of lard into his arms. "*What* does she feed this horse?" he muttered for Susan's ears only. She chuckled and Catherine Elizabeth promptly gave him a big ole lick across the jaw, as if telling him not to worry.

"Oh, look, my baby likes you," Mrs. Abernathy called as she swung the door open wide.

"Seems that way," he grunted. Reaching the car, he leaned in and placed the dog gently into the backseat. She immediately settled into a spot worn into the imprint of her body.

"Can I help you?" He held out one hand to Mrs. Abernathy after gently closing the door on that…dog.

Mrs. Abernathy batted her eyes at him and blushed. "You are such a catch, young man." She slipped her hand into his. She looked at Susan. "If you were smart you'd snatch this one up before someone else puts a ring on that blank finger of his."

Susan surprised him by not looking insulted at the notion. Instead she smiled patiently at her client. "You take care now. And call me if Catherine Elizabeth gets uncomfortable. That extra dose of meds should help her."

"Thank you, dear," the tiny lady said and

eased behind the steering wheel. "You," she said, squeezing his hand before releasing it, "have made my old heart's day!"

"And you have made mine," he said. "You be careful."

She gave him a mischievous smirk. "What fun would that be? Bye now."

He laughed and moved out of her way to stand beside Susan. They watched as the big Crown Victoria eased out of the drive. Mrs. Abernathy's little blue head could barely be seen over the dash and was totally hidden from behind.

"How does she drive a car that big?"

Susan laughed. "Carefully."

"Thank goodness. I half expected her to blast out of here on two wheels."

Susan beamed. "There was probably a day when she did exactly that. Arthur's put a damper on that, I'm afraid."

"Not on her spirit, though, I can see," he said, suddenly feeling rascally himself. "So, you gonna take her advice and marry me before someone else does?"

He was kidding. Susan knew he was, but the question took her completely by surprise. "Of course," she said, turning to face him.

"I've been waiting on you my whole life," she teased back, momentarily letting her guard down.

A slow, dangerous smile spread across his no-way-should-he-be-so-handsome face and his eyes lit with mischief. "You did a joke. Sleep agrees with you, Miss Worth."

She laughed. "I guess it does. But don't go rubbing it in or I'll have to hurt you," she said, before she thought about what a bad idea it was. And it was. She glanced away, toward her truck, taking a breath to settle the strumming of her heart. "Thanks for bringing my truck back." She headed inside the clinic before she got herself into trouble. The scrape of his boots on the wooden porch said he was following her. "I'm assuming you aren't still holding it hostage and you're actually going to hand the keys over to me."

His low rumble of laughter had her moving faster to get inside and behind the counter. She needed a barrier between them—she'd enjoyed watching him with Mrs. Abernathy and Catherine Elizabeth a little too much. The man was a charmer.

And *bossy,* she reminded herself.

And a rover with no concept of responsibility…*not a man for her.*

"Truck's all yours," he said, leaning a hip against the counter. "It checked out good. No undercarriage damage at all. Just a whole herd of dirt clods. The only bad working part it had last night was a worn-out driver who needs to take better care of herself."

And here we go again! "I was tired," she snapped, letting the pencil she'd picked up fall to the desk. "It happens. Can we drop that?" Of course her anger was welcome because it helped put that much-needed barrier back up.

He cocked a brow and his gaze dropped to the pencil she'd just dropped. He picked it up, then as he studied her, balanced it on his upper lip as a schoolboy might do. *Sigh.* The man looked entirely too cute…and was probably well aware of it. She tapped her boot.

"Well," she snapped again, "are you going to drop it?"

"Nope," he said, causing the pencil to fall. He caught it without looking. "Not unless you admit that you should have taken your safety into consideration. That sleep you got last night did you a world of good, didn't it?"

She'd slept like a rock for four hours, but boy, she hated admitting it to him. "If you must know," she huffed, "Mrs. A. had to knock on my door and wake me up this morning."

"All right! Hit me with five," he whooped and held up his palm. "That's good."

She ignored the invitation. "I don't like oversleeping."

He wiggled his fingers. "C'mon. Hit me with some love."

Huh? "No! Would you stop?"

He shook his head, reached across the counter and wrapped his fingers around her wrist. His touch was gentle and as the slightly rough pads of his fingers slid across her skin she shivered. Startled by his actions and her reaction she started to pull away, but he held firm and laid her palm against his.

"There, that wasn't so hard," he said. "You need to loosen up, Susan Worth."

Tugging free of his grasp, she hoped she wasn't pink and that she didn't look as shaken as she felt. "You need to mind your own business," she ordered.

He slapped his hand to his chest. "Wow, what a blow. And after all I've done for you."

"Look," she offered, needing to get him gone. The sooner he was out of her hair the better off she'd be. "I've got a couple more patients to see this morning and then I'm heading out to Clint Matlock's ranch for the rest of the afternoon. I could give you a ride back, but not before then. Unless, of course, you've already arranged a ride." Something told her she wouldn't be so lucky.

"Thanks. I'll wait for you. Unless you need me to hoist more obese dogs into cars—I hope all your clients aren't that large."

Despite herself, a smile tugged at her lips. "I've given up trying to get Catherine Elizabeth on a diet. Mrs. A. has no one else to cook for, and from what I understand, Herman loved to eat. So she can't help but spoil poor Catherine Elizabeth."

Cole did a biceps curl, flexing his muscle for her. "She liked my guns. How about you? I mean, since you have agreed to marry me, what do you think?"

She grunted. "I think you need to go sit down and read a magazine."

"Yup. Just as I thought. You are side-stepping the question because you agree with Mrs. A."

Oh, she agreed—the man had some muscles. Probably from all that construction work he did. But she wasn't about to tell him.

She was relieved when the sound of a motor drew her to glance out the window at the truck pulling up outside. She sent up a silent word of thanks that she could get to work and hopefully get her head straightened out…because it was playing in dangerous waters at the moment. She was moving to Mule Hollow for more reasons than her work. She was moving there with the intention of making room in her life for a husband. That meant flirting with inappropriate men, like Cole, was out of the question.

Now, she thought as she met Cole's watchful stare, if only God would suddenly zap the handsome rover back to wherever it was he'd been before he'd ridden into town last night, she'd be one happy gal.

A man like Cole was not hard to read. He had no plans to settle down; it was all about his job—a job he loved. The ranch he owned with his two brothers had started out as a stagecoach stop—Cole's roots ran six generations deep and yet of the Turner men, including a first cousin who had also been a groomsman in Seth's wedding, Seth was the only one who'd actually stayed true to those roots by keeping the ranch going.

Susan wanted a family. Her mind was

focused on that, and yet she still had to keep her business running. Her dad had cared so much about her having a career, wanting his little girl to be able to take care of herself. She'd done that, but now she had to find a way of balancing family with her work. She knew that meant she had to find a man who would complement her life. So even looking at a rover like Cole was out of the question.

She walked around the edge of the counter and forced herself not to make a wide arc around him. Instead she stopped beside him and glanced at his "guns." "Actually, Mrs. A. has a great point. But in reality it'll take a bunch more than that to interest me."

The door opened and she hurried to usher the prancing pack of toy poodles into the exam room. The owner was so flustered trying to hang on to four leashes at once that she didn't even give Cole a glance. Susan, however, paused to note Cole had taken the first seat in the small waiting area.

"Whatever you say, but I'm here," he said, flexing his muscle for her. "If you need me, you just call."

She shook her head and closed the door with a resounding thud. She needed Cole Turner the way she needed a hole in the head!

Chapter Four

"So what's up, brother?"

Cole opened his eyes and found his brother Seth leaning against the door, grinning.

"Thought I'd swing by and welcome you home, since I heard through the grapevine you'd arrived."

After Susan had dropped him off at his truck, Cole drove back to the stagecoach house, walked inside and crashed on the couch. It had been a long time since he'd slept. "Sorry I didn't come by. What time is it?" he asked, rubbing his jaw as he swung his legs around and plopped his feet to the ground. He felt like he'd been run over by a truck. This was most likely how Susan had been feeling last night when she'd run off the road.

"It's five. And from App and Stanley's account it sounds like you've been busy since arriving last night."

Cole gave him a groggy nod. Good ole Applegate and Stanley. "Yeah, you could say so. Susan's going to love knowing everyone in town knows she fell asleep at the wheel."

"That's the honest truth," Seth grunted. "You look like the dickens, bro." Seth strode into the kitchen, separated from the living room by only an ancient dining table.

"Feel like it, too."

"You could have given me a call. I would have come and helped out." He grabbed the coffeepot and began filling it with water.

"Yeah, with the cell-phone coverage Mule Hollow has I'd have been wasting my time."

"True, but the phone here works and I could have at least picked you up after you drove Susan's truck to the clinic."

"Believe me, as hot as I was at you this morning—you wanted me to get some shut-eye before you saw me." That drew Seth's attention. "What were you thinking letting that woman leave your barn in the shape she was in last night?" Cole stood up and felt his blood pressure rise thinking about Susan barreling toward those trees as he'd topped the hill. "She was so tired she very nearly got herself killed falling asleep at the wheel."

"For starters, one doesn't tell a man how to run his business. Same goes for Susan. She's worked hard to get where she is with her business and she doesn't take kindly to being separated out. She assured me she was fine—"

It was the same thing App and Stanley said. Still, Cole pointed out, "She looked like death warmed over—"

"Hey, I took her at her word. Like I would have a man in that situation. Didn't say I liked it, but that's the way she wants it."

Cole padded angrily into the kitchen, not willing to take that as an excuse. "She wasn't fine. She was dead on her feet. She'd been up three nights in a row. Did you know that?"

"Yeah, I did," Seth snapped, jabbing the on button to the coffeepot before swinging to face him.

"Then what were you thinking? You would have been responsible if—"

"Now just hold on, Cole. I hate that she had to work that much, but it couldn't be helped. None of us call her out like that unless absolutely necessary. I'd have had a dead cow and calf this morning if not for her efforts last night. If I'd let them die so she could get some sleep, Susan would have taken it as a slap in the face. You know good and well she's my friend, but we tread a fine line where Susan is concerned."

Cole rubbed his aching neck and told himself to back down. He didn't like it, but he also knew his brother. Seth was level-headed and kind, and Susan really was his friend. "Sorry, I get your drift," he grumbled, still frustrated. "But it'd sure be a shame if something happened to her."

Seth nodded and his serious expression said he was sincere. "We'll all rest easier when Susan gets moved into town. Did she tell you about all that?"

"Yeah, she told me. *Only* after I asked her. Applegate told me she was moving into town this morning—or Stanley. One of the fellas did—their conversation ran together in my brain."

Seth looked amused. "App and Stanley's conversations tend to run together even on a good night's sleep."

"You have a point." They both chuckled, easing the tension.

"So how long are you here for? I'm here

to wake you up and haul your sorry hide back over to the house so Melody can interrogate you. But it should be a fair trade since she's hard at work cookin' up a meal fit for a king."

Cole took the cup of coffee Seth handed him and held it aloft. "Then let me drink this, and then I'll hop in the shower so I'm presentable to my new sister-in-law. I already have one hometown gal irritated with me, I wouldn't want to make that sweet bride of yours unhappy with me, too. How'd you get so lucky anyway?"

"Not lucky, but blessed, thanks to the good Lord and Wyatt."

Cole took a swig of coffee. "Our big bro the matchmaker. Never in a thousand years would I have expected that six-foot-four-inch hunk of hot air to be a little Cupid!"

That got a big laugh from Seth. "Boy, does that paint some kind of picture!"

Cole grimaced. "True. Still, it is amazing that he met Melody one day and knew she was the match for you." He cocked a brow at Seth, who reciprocated. It had been a weird thing when Wyatt met Melody and decided instantly to have her do some research on the family history. History that Seth hadn't wanted researched. It had thrown the two of them into a battle of wills and then into a hunt for long-lost treasure.

"Wyatt wouldn't be such a great lawyer unless he was good at reading people," Seth mused. "Maybe that was it."

Cole didn't know what it was, but serious, levelheaded Seth was happier and more relaxed than Cole had thought possible. He deserved it. "You look good, Seth," he said, drawing his own thoughts away from Lori. Thoughts of how happy they could have been if things hadn't been…the way they'd been.

"I am happy. Melody—"

"Completes you," Cole teased with the famous movie line, forcing the door to his past shut.

"You laugh, but it's so true."

"I'm not laughing. I like it. Wyatt might have missed his calling."

"Maybe he'll do the same for you."

"Oh, no," Cole said. "I've got places to be and things to see. I'm not settling down—but it sure looks good on you."

"So, any clues why Wyatt wanted you home or what he had to do to get you here? What's up with that?"

"He said he'd tell me when he showed up tomorrow." Cole set his coffee down and headed toward the hall, tugging his shirt up over his head as he went. "But *I* came because I decided it was time to come see how married life was treatin' you."

"Well, in that case it should be clear that I'm doin' well."

Cole halted at the doorway to the hall. "I can see that, but I want to get a gander at Melody and make sure she's got the same goofy grin on her face. I'll be out in a minute."

"Cole, hold up a minute. About Susan."

"What about her?"

"I'm guessing you're in town for a short visit and, well, you should know Susan is looking for a real relationship. One that includes a future and a family. I hope you keep that in mind while you're here."

Cole shot Seth a warning look. "I didn't come back here to break any hearts, if that's what you're worried about. I'm here and then I'm back on the road. I've got places to be."

"Look, Cole, I didn't mean it like that. It's been six years. I'm actually hoping you're ready to settle down and think—"

"Don't go there, Seth," Cole warned, an edge to his voice that had Seth setting his coffee down and frowning at him in disappointment. He pushed away from the counter and stood staring at Cole. The tension between them was born of love and concern. Still, Cole hadn't come home for more lectures on the life he'd chosen.

He turned and headed to the bathroom. Truth was, he didn't really have a clue why he'd come home. Sure Wyatt had forced him in a way Seth would never know about…but even with that, Cole hadn't had to come. So why had he?

Okay, just calm down! "What do you mean you're going on an extended hunt in Alaska?"

Susan was behind the counter at Sam's diner talking on the diner phone. The cell reception in Mule Hollow was extremely scarce so she often had to use client landlines to keep in touch with Betty, her part-time receptionist, back at the office. Today she'd expected to meet her contractor out at the new property so they could go over plans before he started working. He hadn't shown. After waiting an hour she'd driven into town to use Sam's phone.

Betty had given her the distressing news that her contractor had quit. *Quit!* He couldn't quit. She'd immediately dialed him up.

"Just what I said," the louse drawled. "I'm *goin'* to Alaska."

Susan turned her back to the diner, lowering her voice so as not to shout to the small crowd in the diner. She didn't want everyone to know she had trouble. "You said I was next in line," she said, using great restraint. Her daddy always told her to keep a lid on her temper, that a ranting woman didn't get any respect from a man, but…she was so mad she could spit nails! "We had a deal."

"Look, lady, I got a better deal. An offer I couldn't refuse, so to speak. I'm outta here on the fishing trip of a lifetime."

An offer he couldn't refuse. Where did he get such an offer? "So, let me get this straight. Your word means nothing."

His next words were not nice. And being told in no uncertain terms that she was "up a creek without a paddle" did not help her mood.

If the guy quit for a better job she might not be so furious. But, no, the man was going fishing. *Fishing!*

Fighting down the urge to kick something, Susan carefully hung the wall phone in its cradle. It took all she had not to slam it down.

Now what?

She bit her lip and stared hard at the phone.

What was she going to do? The interior of her new office space needed walls torn out and new ones built. Counters and shelves, not to mention the electric wiring and plumbing required updates, too. And it all had to be done by the end of the month. She could hear her dad's calm voice reminding her to keep her cool, buckle down, and get the job done. "Getting the job done was what mattered," he'd say, in that Texas twang that still made her smile to think of it. Still made her miss him like crazy. Still made her want to please him. And she would. She'd had setbacks before and his words always drove her to get it done.

Right now she had to get her appointments finished for the day and get home. If she was lucky tonight, she'd get a full night's sleep and be ready to tackle finding a new contractor tomorrow. She was still working on fumes from exhaustion. If tonight went without an emergency call she'd get the much-needed sleep and wipe out the fog of exhaustion clouding her head. But lately it seemed like emergency calls were non-stop.

"Here's your burger, Doc," Sam said, coming out of the back with a paper bag in his hand. His sharp old eyes seemed to look through her. "Every thang okay? You look kinda pink."

"Everything's fine, Sam—" She bit her lip. "Actually that's not true. You wouldn't happen to know a good contractor, would you?"

Sam was a tiny man in his mid- to late-sixties with the boundless energy of a man much younger. He was a hard worker like her dad had been and she respected him greatly. He also knew everyone within a hundred-mile radius of town.

He scrubbed his chin. "Contractors. You got trouble?"

"Looks that way. I need to get moved in before my contract deadline gets here in three weeks. But," she practically growled the word, "my guy just hung me out to dry. He said he got offered a fishing trip. *A fishing trip.* And is going fishing in Alaska."

Sam grimaced, his weathered face wrinkling. "Tank Clawson always was one ta put play b'fore work. It's a wonder the man kin afford ta finance all his vacations."

Susan knew what it was. Supply and demand paid well. The man did good work when he did it and people were willing to pay him top dollar. She'd hired him because he'd said he could fit her in between two big jobs that were scheduled. "I didn't get the impression that he was paying for this trip."

Sam tugged on his ear. "That's purdy odd."

"Yes, sir, it is. Thanks for the lunch, Sam. What would I do without you?"

His brows dipped. "You'd dry up and wither away. You need ta slow down, sit in one of them thar booths and eat that burger on the sit-down rather than on the blamed run. If you did that, one of them cowboys might sit down with you and who knows where that would lead."

She glanced toward the tables and the three different tables full of cowboys. She was going to do that soon as she got settled. "No time today. I've wasted more time than I had to give. I still have a load of cattle to see at Clint's place and that's going to take all afternoon." She grabbed the bag and waggled it at him. "Thanks again."

He scowled. "It ain't no wonder Cole Turner had to rescue ya out of that ditch. It's a wonder you didn't fall asleep sooner and get yourself killed."

"Sam, I'm trying to slow down. If I can get a contractor out there working, the sooner I'll get to sleep more."

"I'm on it."

"Thanks. I'm sure if there is a contractor out there to be found, you'll find him—or you'll help me find someone who knows one."

"Yup. I might jest have a good 'un in mind already."

"Really?" Susan's hopes shot up. "Who?"

"Can't say just yet. You comin' to the barbecue tomorrow night at Clint and Lacy's ranch, aren't you?"

"Yes," Susan said, wondering who he had in mind. "Are you?"

"Yup. Got my relief cook lined up fer this place. Me and Adela will see you thar." He nodded. "Probably gonna be an interesting night since Cole will be thar, too."

Just what she'd been afraid of—the man was going to start turning up all over the place. There would be nowhere to hide until he got bored and left. "He won't be around long from what I've heard about him," she said, and then wished she'd just taken her burger and hit the road as planned.

"Maybe." Sam slapped his ever-present dish towel over his shoulder with a grin. "And maybe not."

Chapter Five

Cole's gaze swept over the gathering as he trailed behind Seth and Melody toward the backyard barbecue. Clint and Lacy Matlock had a beautiful ranch. The main house sat on a hill and overlooked a stunning valley.

It wasn't the view that had Cole's attention, however, it was the tall beauty leaning against the deck banister watching him.

He'd wondered if she was going to be here. As much as they had a weird kind of thing going on, he realized the minute he saw her that he'd been hoping to see her.

As he passed a tub of iced-down sodas he grabbed two and headed her way. Maybe he should have stayed back, but that wasn't part of his makeup. Even if she didn't look happy to see him.

He mounted the steps. "Don't look so hostile, Doc. I come with soda." He popped the top of a can and handed it to her; she didn't take it. "Come on now, it would be rude to snub your handsome rescuer."

She reluctantly accepted the drink. "You are going to milk that accident for all it's worth, aren't you?"

"Maybe." He opened his drink and took a swig. "I have to say, I'm pretty good at reading people, but you are a puzzle."

"How so?"

"Despite my being your knight in shining armor, I continually get the feeling that you'd as soon see me run over by wild horses."

Susan almost choked on her soda. "I do not."

She had added a touch of shimmer to her lips and now she clamped those pretty lips together. It was a warm day for April but the temperature edged up a few more degrees as they stared at each other. "Oh, you know it's true."

"For your information, I know you aren't going to be in town long. So, I—"

"How do you know?"

"Well, um…you never come home much."

The good doctor was flustered. "Have you been checking up on me, Doc?"

"No. Of course not."

Call him crazy for flirting—and he was, but he was enjoying himself. He was about to press further when Norma Sue Jenkins rounded the corner of the house and spotted him.

"Cole Turner," she bellowed and engulfed him in a bear hug. The short, stout woman practically lifted him from the deck in her enthusiasm.

"You are a sight for sore eyes!" Norma Sue declared. She was married to Clint Matlock's foreman, Roy Don. She and Roy Don had been friends of his grandparents and his parents. As a boy he and his brothers had spent almost as many evenings at Roy Don and Norma Sue's house as their own. Norma was pure robust Texas cattlewoman from the tip of her boots to the top of her white Stetson. She'd always worn jeans and pearl-button, Western shirts or blue bibbed overalls—except on Sunday when she was partial to striped dresses. Tonight she'd chosen jeans and a pale blue, pearl-button shirt. Her kinky gray hair poked out from beneath the Stetson and tickled his jaw when she yanked his head to her shoulder and smothered him as if she hadn't seen him in years.

Norma Sue had always been a big hugger

and he'd hated it as a kid. But as a man who often missed his parents and grandparents, he enjoyed the comfort her hugs always gave him. "I missed you, boy," she said, finally releasing him.

"Norma Sue, I saw you at the wedding, so if you keep this up folks are gonna start talking."

She slapped him on the arm and frowned. "I'm gearing up for when you leave town and don't come back again for years. Like *before Seth's wedding*," she said accusingly. "I can't believe you came home twice in the same year."

Roy Don had come over and now reached in for a quick fatherly hug of his own. "Welcome home, son. She gets plumb mad when she thinks about you off running the roads and not having enough time to come home. I didn't hardly have any peace after you rode off into the sunset only hours after the reception."

"Sorry about that." Cole had planned on staying around longer after the wedding, but as happy as he'd been for Seth and Melody, emotions he hadn't expected had slammed into him during the evening. He'd had no choice but to leave. He'd been in a blue mood for weeks afterward.

He'd been furious with God after Lori, and it had taken him a long time to regain some kind of relationship with his God. Just like the relationship between father and son can be strained, so had his become with his heavenly Father. But as a father and son reconciled so he had been trying. Unexpectedly Seth's wedding had almost taken him back to square one.

There was no way he'd ever want Seth or Melody to know that…Wyatt, on the other hand had figured it out—not that he'd figured it out completely, but still…that was Cole's reason for being here now. His big brother had decided it was time for Cole to come home for an extended visit and had threatened to tell Seth all if he didn't cooperate and return. Wyatt reasoned that if Cole came home and spent time with the newlyweds it would help him get over his past. Cole didn't want to get over his past…and that, Wyatt had argued, was the problem.

"Now—" Roy Don grinned beneath his wide mustache "—you can well imagine my *delight* to hear you were coming back for a visit so soon."

Cole chuckled at the old cowboy's use of the word *delight*. "I'm glad it's helped you out."

Norma Sue beamed, her round cheeks so tight they shined in the dwindling sunlight. "Two times in one year, that's a record. And a long time coming." She glanced at Susan. "We're hoping maybe he'll stay."

"I see." Susan's skeptical, blue gaze hit him full force before dropping to the can of soda.

Something about the look he'd just seen had Cole stumbling over a reply. "I've been real busy," he said, yanking his gaze from Susan's and meeting Norma's hawk eyes. The woman's brain was clicking along as she studied him and Susan. "Unfortunately there's been lots of rebuilding needed along the Gulf Coast." He needed to get this conversation back on track and fast.

"We know you've been doing great things," Norma Sue said, jumping on board.

"You represent your hometown very well," Roy Don chimed in. "Don't you ever forget how proud we are to call you our own."

"That's right," Norma Sue agreed. "We're just glad to get to see you. We can't help but hope you settle down here with a nice girl who'll give you lots of babies." Her gaze slid toward Susan and his followed—like an idiot. Susan's eyes flared but she did a great job holding her expression neutral.

He swallowed hard and hoped he did as good a job. "I'm not really lookin—"

Norma broke in and slapped him on the back. "We're sure glad you were there for our Susan. God knew what He was doing when He had you there to help her. At exactly the right moment—isn't that something. I tell you, I *do* believe in God's timing."

Susan's eyes widened. If it hadn't been so off base for him he might have found her reaction funny. Norma Sue never had been one for beating around the bush.

"Now, Norma, don't go thinking of match-making me," he warned. Norma Sue and her two best friends, Esther Mae Wilcox and Sam's wife, Adela, were eaten up with match-making. They'd saved the town from drying up and blowing away by coming up with the idea to advertise for wives. They'd found their calling, that was for sure. The proof stood around the yard—most all of the couples at the ranch tonight had been matched up by them in some way.

"Cole!"

The shriek came from Esther Mae Wilcox as she emerged from the house carrying a big bowl of fruit. She plopped it down on the long table then hustled his way. Esther was as loud in person as she was in attire. She wore purple-and-pink-striped calf-length pants and a purple shirt with a humongous pink rose across one entire side. It was as bright pink as her hair was brilliant red. Her personality was just as vibrant.

"About time I got a hug. I heard you were back in town." She threw her arms around him.

"Esther Mae, how in the world are you?" he asked. When he was five he'd been squirming to get away at this point. "Is that Hank still treatin' you right or are you ready to run away with me?"

Esther Mae giggled and stepped away. She was a tinge of pink herself. "You always were a charmer—you and Wyatt got that direct from the Turner side."

"True, but the offer stands."

She elbowed him. "My Hank wouldn't know what to do if I ran away."

"I know that's the truth." He laughed.

"Our forty-year wedding anniversary is tomorrow."

Norma Sue gave everyone a comical grimace. "You two are sure getting old, Esther Mae."

"Hey, don't try that. You and Roy Don are coming up on forty-three years."

"True, but I was a baby when we got married."

"So was I." Esther Mae giggled. "That's my story and I'm sticking to it."

Cole chuckled and his gaze slid toward Susan. He was startled at the wistful look in her eyes as she stared at Esther Mae.

"That's wonderful, Esther Mae. I'm so happy for you two," she said. "Um, I need to head inside. I told Lacy I'd help her."

Cole watched her leave. This evening was good for her. She wasn't working; she didn't look tired. On the contrary, she looked fantastic. Yet there was something about her that didn't seem right. And he couldn't help but wonder what that something was.

"Lacy!" Susan entered the kitchen and was relieved to find her friend alone. She'd just finished icing a cake and was running her finger along the rim of the bowl of leftover icing.

"What's up, girlfriend? You look like you've seen Elvis or something."

"I wish! It's Norma Sue and Esther Mae. I think they're up to something. I see it in their eyes."

Lacy plopped her icing-covered finger into her mouth on her way to the sink with the knife and bowl. "I hate to break it to you, but you're right on target with that. This afternoon they came into the salon buzzing like bees," she confided, grimacing. "Cole's coming home has put a sparkle in their eyes and you know what that means. Adela's in the back room rocking Dottie's baby to sleep, but believe me, she's on the same page with her cohorts. The matchmaking posse is locked and loaded."

Susan bit her lip. "Any idea what they're locked on to?"

"They're determined to get Cole to stay home. They're looking for a match for that hunk of hometown cowboy, convinced falling in love will do the deed."

Dread filled Susan. "But he's not looking to stay."

"A man can change his mind."

"Well, yes, but he just seems like he loves the road."

"The road gets old. Or so they say." Lacy picked up the cake and beamed at her. The petite blonde's blue eyes sparkled with mischief. "You worried about something?"

"N-no. I mean, the man doesn't mean anything to me." Susan meant it, too.

"You two sure sound like y'all have hit it off."

"Oh, no, we haven't."

Lacy laughed. "That cowboy had you in his sights the minute he got out of his truck and headed toward this house. And you zeroed in on him just as quickly."

"That is so not true. And besides, you weren't even outside."

"Ha! I was looking out the window. The temperature went up twenty degrees."

"Lacy Matlock, you better back up right now. Do not put any ideas in the matchmakers' heads. I'm your basic homebody tied to my job and he lives on a Harley. He and I just don't compute as a match."

"That is just typical Susan Work-and-No-Play Worth," Lacy practically sang. "I thought you were moving here to have a social life. The gals have that in mind for you, so relax, get to know the guy. Have a little faith."

Susan felt hot. Hot as in get-sick hot. *Cole Turner*—no way.

No matter how attractive she found Cole Turner he wasn't the one for her. The risk was too great where he was concerned.

Faith was good to have, but God didn't just give people good heads on their shoulders. He put a brain inside, too. If she threw caution to the wind and let the ladies match her with a rolling stone, she'd be crazy.

She was startled when Lacy sobered and suddenly hugged her.

"It's okay," she said. "You know the gals well enough to know they only want the best for you, right?"

"I know what's best for me and it isn't Cole Turner."

Lacy hooted at that and it didn't make Susan feel very confident as Lacy tugged her toward the door. "You are about the wariest gal I ever saw. It's time to eat, Susan. But remember that sometimes God does open others' eyes to things to give us little nudges in the right direction."

"I've got a great sense of direction and that's why I'm staying as far away from Cole as I can get while he's in town."

Lacy glanced over her shoulder as she led the way outside. "Whatever you say. But I've got a feeling it won't be that easy."

Oh, yes, it would be, Susan thought as she stepped out onto the deck and practically ran into Sam.

"Just the woman I been lookin' fer," he said, grabbing her by the arm. "You still needin' a contractor?"

"Yes," she said, feeling relief just from the enthusiasm she heard in his voice. Getting the work started on her clinic would take some of the pressure off her. "Did you find someone already?"

"Yup, shor did. Come with me." He tucked her arm into the crook of his wiry arm and headed across the deck.

The crowd around Cole had grown and that was the direction Sam was taking her. She studied the group and knew none of them were contractors. *"Sam,"* she said, slowing her steps.

"Now, don't go gettin' cold feet," he said, coming to a halt in front of Cole. Cole looked from her to Sam.

"Cole." Sam grinned. "Susan has a proposal for ya."

Chapter Six

"A proposal?"

Cole's smoky-blue eyes deepened with warm curiosity as he crossed his arms and studied Susan. Unbelievably, for that moment she felt as if she was the only person standing near him. It was as disturbing as the past three minutes had been.

"Yup," Sam quipped, pushing Susan forward a step. "Susan's got the perfect job for you while yor home."

Susan wanted to crawl under a rock, but everyone was looking at her. She fought to look calm and collected.

"And what would that be?" Cole drawled, shifting his weight against the deck railing he was leaning against.

"Yesterday her contractor left her high and

dry when he quit on her. She's in a bind and needs a good contractor—you'd be perfect for the job."

Perfect for the job! Oh, what a nightmare.

Cole straightened, looking as startled as she felt. "Do you really need some help?" he asked, sounding as if he'd like her to say no.

She couldn't say no, not with the whole town listening. "Yes, but I'm sure you wouldn't have time for something like that. This was Sam's idea. Sam," she said, turning her attention to the older man, "he's here to visit with Seth and Melody before he goes back to work." There, she'd given him the perfect out. Maybe he'd take the hint and hit the road sooner.

"Actually—"

Just the way he drew the word out had her every nerve on full alert as her gaze shot back to meet his.

"I could come out and take a look."

Talk about blowing her plan to stay away from him to smithereens. She couldn't allow this to happen…and yet she was needed in her clinic.

"But only if you wanted me to," he added when she said nothing.

"That is a great idea," Lacy called from the

back of the crowd. Susan shot her a glare and caught the twinkle of laughter in her eyes.

"So perfect!" exclaimed Esther Mae.

"No," Susan blurted out. She couldn't even consider this. No matter how desperate she was.

"But it is the perfect solution," Norma Sue admonished, looking at her as though she was crazy for even considering saying no to the darling of Mule Hollow.

This was absolutely unbelievable. Her only consolation was that she realized Cole looked as conflicted as she was. That was slightly comforting in an odd sort of way. *Slightly.*

"Let him take a look," Applegate said, stepping out from somewhere in the crowd. She hadn't even seen him until that moment. "You ain't never been a fool where business was concerned, so don't start now."

She shot him an indignant glare, no longer able to control her displeasure at this entire idea.

Cole cocked his head to the side. "You want me to take a look?"

Boy, was this crazy. "Sure," she snapped, feeling outnumbered. "If you've got the time that would be… fine."

"He's got the time," Seth said from beside Applegate. "Me and Melody will be glad for him to do anything that will prolong his visit."

It was Cole's turn to aim a quizzical expression at his brother. "You just tell me when and where and I'll be there to take a gander at what you've got."

Susan's heart sank. She took a deep breath and gave a tiny nod. It took all she had to make her chin move down and up.

"Take him over thar now," Sam declared. "You don't need to be hem-hawin' around. This clinic business needs ta get goin' as soon as possible and this here barbecue will still be here when y'all get back."

"Now?" Susan gasped before she caught herself.

Cole chuckled. "Sure. Now sounds good to me. Lacy, we'll be back before the hour is up. Is that okay?"

"Yep, yep, yep," she sang in true Lacy fashion. "Take all the time you need. You know my parties just keep going."

Susan could only hold in her dismay as Cole stepped forward and took her arm. His fingers were warm and sent tingles dancing across skin as he guided her toward his truck.

Suddenly she found herself in the same situation as the night of the accident when he'd taken over…railroaded once more.

"This is ridicul—"

"Hold on," Cole murmured close to her ear as they walked. "This is the easiest way. If you don't go with the flow, you won't hear the end of it all night."

He was right and she knew it.

Yes, she was being railroaded all right. But this time it was by the entire town! What in the world was she going to do?

Cole was trying to ignore the obvious matchmaking endeavor they'd just witnessed as he closed the passenger door to his truck and headed around to his side.

He climbed in with a quick glance at his passenger then concentrated on getting them on the road and away from prying eyes and calculating minds!

His friends wanted him back home and it was obvious that this was how they planned to do it. He'd expected to stay in town long enough to make Wyatt drop this sudden interest in his life and well-being. He hadn't expected this.

A couple of days was what he'd hoped it

would take. Wyatt had said he was going to join him here and he'd planned to leave soon after. But his big brother, in true Wyatt form, had called this afternoon and said it would be Wednesday or Thursday before he could make it to town. His case load was too full and he couldn't get away. That was almost a week away. So Cole had agreed to stay until then.

Now oddly enough he was intrigued by the whole aspect of what had just transpired. The fact that he was intrigued and not mad about it was weird. But if Susan was worried about him getting the wrong idea then she didn't have anything to be concerned about. Nope, intrigued or not, he wasn't here to fall in love—as it was so obvious his little match-making hometown friends were envisioning. Susan could rest easy on that point. He wasn't lookin' for love.

"So your contractor left you hanging?" he asked finally, when she made no attempt at conversation.

"Yes. He got an offer he couldn't refuse. Chose to go fishing in Alaska. Some people's work ethic amazes me."

"On that we agree." Cole shot her an agree-able glance. Even in disasters he was amazed at how men would walk off from jobs and leave folks in the lurch. Folks who'd already suffered enough pain when their houses had been destroyed by acts of God… He knew how they felt in a way. He'd lost Lori due to a lack of action on God's part—he pushed that out of his head. "Someone with a work ethic like yours *would* feel that way." Instantly he felt her eyes drill into him and he decided keeping his eyes on the road was the smart thing.

"I believe in working hard," she said. There was a defensive edge in her words. "Being dedicated to what I do. And being there when my clients—who *rely* on me—need me."

"Calm down," he urged, meeting her glare. "I didn't say it was a bad thing. I admire your dedication."

Two bright spots of pink appeared on her cheeks. "Oh, sorry. I didn't mean to be so touchy. It's just, well, not everyone feels that way."

They'd reached the crossroads and he pulled the truck to a halt before turning the direction of the clinic. "I'm sure in your business being a bit touchy comes in handy. You probably have to stand your ground."

He caught a flicker of emotion in her eyes that he'd glimpsed momentarily when she'd been exhausted. Vulnerability wasn't her style but it was there and he knew instinctively that she hated it. Saw it as weakness.

"Yes, I do," she said, rubbing her thigh as if the idea worried her.

The deep sigh that followed the statement seemed to go unnoticed by her and he wondered if she'd even realized she'd done it. He couldn't help being curious about her. Wondered if there was something in particular that drove her. "It's this way, right?" he asked, knowing it was, but wanting to give her something else to think about.

"Yes, about five miles out."

He drove as she gave him more detailed directions and related who it had belonged to. All stuff he'd already garnered from Applegate and Stanley. "That'll be a perfect spot for your business. I guess that place has sat empty for years now?"

"Yes. I'm excited. But you don't have to do this."

He smiled and meant it. "I know. But I can at least take a look for you."

An uncomfortable silence settled between them. He chose not to press. He was a quick study, and it didn't take a genius to figure out that Susan hated to be pressed.

Tonight he didn't want to fight. Glancing at her, he realized he wanted to get to know her better. Despite their ability to rub each other the wrong way, they did have a few things in common.

"There it is," she said the instant it came into view.

It had weathered well on the outside; since it was a metal building he'd expected as much. But the rutted drive would need some attention before horse trailers and an abundance of traffic started in on it. "You picked a good spot," he commented as he pulled to a stop.

"Thanks. It's a bit off the beaten path, but so is everything else around here."

She opened her door and hopped from the truck before he could say more. He watched her stride to the front door first, then he followed. It was easy to tell she was uncomfortable being in close proximity to him. But she was excited about her place, though she seemed to be downplaying it a bit.

A sense of challenge overtook him as he moved toward her. Who was Susan Worth? All kinds of questions had been popping up in his head about her lately. What drove her? Why was she so determined to hide the flicker of softness he'd glimpsed briefly both today and the other night? Those and other questions surged, but he pushed them away as he followed. He was here to look at her building…not play fill in the blank with the doc.

The building was like most of the older metal buildings—white corrugated sheet metal with faded blue trim around the windows and along the roofline. The metal front door was dull gray with no window and a large dent at the bottom as if it had been kicked.

There were two large windows on either side of the door, so that would at least let light into what he assumed would be the waiting area. She unlocked the door and led the way into the large open room. In the business of assessing damage and fixing it, for insurance claims or for emergency situations, he was used to walking into buildings and automatically evaluating the situation.

"Not too bad," he said, as his gaze took in the cheap paneling in the room. He glanced out the door that led into the back area where oil rig fittings and pipes had once been kept. "At least it has good bones."

She tucked her fingers into the fronts of her jeans and rocked onto her toes. "It does, doesn't it?"

The excitement in her voice was unmistakable. What was up with that? Was it just to him that she was trying to appear subdued?

"So what do you want to do in here?"

"As you can tell, this room is too small and that back area is too big. I need a reception area built and then exam rooms. Also an office and a records area. Plus holding area and surgery. And a dispensary. Something similar to what I have in Ranger."

"Good idea. How many exam rooms?"

"At least two. And I'll want the surgery to be larger than what I have now."

As he'd hoped she would, she began to loosen up, tugging her fingers from her pockets she began using her hands to help describe where and how she wanted things constructed. Moving about the room and out into the back area she elaborated on her vision for the space. He kept his comments to a minimum, only offering suggestions occasionally.

When she finally finished she spun toward him. "So, that's about it. I know it's a lot and my problem is I need it done by the end of the month. My buyer at the Ranger clinic wants to take over the first day of May. I had agreed originally because my contractor assured me it could be done—there was no fishing trip in the picture. Now, I'm not sure. What do you think? Could it be done?"

"Yes."

"Is this something you might really be interested in taking on?" she asked with a mixture of uncertainty and wistfulness all rolled into one sweet expression. His heart twisted remembering a similar expression. "He was right. It is doable," he said, modulating his tone to hold steady. This was about Susan. "Given, the amount of work we're looking at it might be tight. I wouldn't delay getting started for much longer." He hadn't answered her question. Did he want to tackle it?

She frowned. "That's what I'm afraid of. And there just aren't that many contractors who want to drive all the way out here to the middle of nowhere. This is cattle country, but there's not a lot of building going on."

Cole had a feeling he was going to live to regret this but he couldn't leave her hanging. He hadn't planned on working construction while he was home. Hadn't planned on staying the four weeks it would take to do this job. "I know I'm the last man you'd want to work with." Might as well put the truth on the table.

"Yes."

He grinned; he couldn't stop it. "Most women would have lied on that one."

"What would be the use in our situation?" she said. "Be honest, this is the last job you'd want. Working for me, while the town tries to figure out how to keep you here."

"Yes," he answered as bluntly as she had. "That said, I'm still offering my services if you want to take me up on the offer." There were all kinds of reasons why he wanted to turn tail and hit the road. But he could help her. He could get her into this building on time and get her dreams heading in the right direction.

The fulfillment of some dreams—other people's dreams—drove him. God hadn't given him the chance or the ability to make his own dream come true. His dream of a life with Lori—of seeing Lori survive her cancer—that had all been out of his hands. But other dreams…dreams that had been dashed through the wrath of Mother Nature— God had granted him the ability to revive.

In doing so, He'd given Cole a reason to keep going. A reason to get up in the mornings.

Susan looked slightly pensive, unsure about him. He didn't have to convey to her that the folks of Mule Hollow would be on a matchmaking tear once she agreed.

She took a deep breath, turned on her heel in a slow swivel as her gaze roamed the office of her dreams. Suddenly she spun back. "When can you start?"

Chapter Seven

"Praise the Lord!" Betty exclaimed on Saturday morning. Susan's receptionist let her half-eaten doughnut hover in front of her mouth as Susan entered the clinic. "You look like you're back in the land of the living. Got some sleep the past couple of nights?"

"Sure did," Susan said, watching as Betty stuffed the rest of the doughnut into her mouth. "You sure you even taste what you're chewing so fast?"

Swiping sugar particles from her lips, Betty grinned. "You should be cramming down a few with the crazy busy day you've got ahead of you. And I do mean crazy! Your tongue's goin' to be dragging before noon!"

Susan glanced down at the book. It had every slot filled in and then more scribbled into the margins. Betty still insisted on using a paper schedule instead of the computer because she couldn't fit folks in—and she always had to fit folks in. "Wow, I tell you, Betty. I'm ready for a rest."

"I've been telling you that you need to slow down. I know your daddy meant well driving you to be a success, but surely he didn't mean for you to be old before your time. And I know your momma wouldn't have wanted this. No mother would want her daughter so caught up in work she couldn't enjoy life."

Susan didn't talk about her mother much, but she had talked with Betty about growing up without a mother. She and her dad had made it, but there had always been that void left by her absence. Knowing her mother had died giving birth to her had made Susan feel horrible growing up. But she'd known her mother loved her dearly. "I know you're right. Since Dad's death I've been thinking about that a lot."

"Good. You need to think about what she'd want and find a husband who'll give you babies and help you in your business."

Susan nodded, hoping such a man was out there for her.

"So what's this I hear about the hunky Cole Turner? I take my three days off and come back to a very disturbing situation."

"How did you know about Cole?"

"Me'n George drove to Mule Hollow on Thursday night for all-you-can-eat catfish at Sam's. Believe me when I say I heard all about your falling asleep and the white-knight rescue. Why, to hear them talk it was straight out of one of them romance novels I read."

Susan cringed at being the talk of the town. It came with the territory when one lived in a small town, but to have everything blown out of proportion like this wasn't good. The reality had hit home at Lacy's when she'd realized she was now the target of the match-making posse. And then, she'd made things worse by giving in to their plans.

Things could only get worse on that front now that she'd done it. Needing sugar, she picked up a doughnut, but put it back down. "Don't believe everything you hear," she said, snatching up the stack of mail and thumbing through it.

"So what is going on? I heard he's the wandering brother. Not the lawyer, though from what I hear he flies all over the place,

too. What is it with these Turner men?" Betty
was talking at the speed of light and didn't
pause after the question. "Only one that
knows how to stay put is Seth... You should
have snatched that one up but quick," she
huffed. "Not go gettin' on the back of this
Cole's Harley. Is it true you did that?"

Susan nodded. "Believe me, I didn't want
to get on the back of that thing, either."

The mother hen in Betty was out as she
crossed her arms and met Susan's gaze. She
took this job seriously. "Flirting around with
a man like that isn't gonna help you find
yourself a husband. That's why you're
moving to Mule Hollow in the first place.
You don't need to be messing around with
someone like this dude. You need a cowboy
who is going to hang around. A Harley," she
harrumphed.

"Boy, aren't you wound up this morning?"
Susan wondered where her first appointment
was. It would help everything if they'd arrive
and she could get to work.

"Hey, I'm all for you moving your practice
so you can have time to find a husband. But
from all accounts this Cole is a good man, but
he's a rover. You need a man who will help
you in this business where possible. *Someone*

who will be there for you. You don't need one off saving the world."

Saving the world. Was that what Cole was doing? "You're right. I agree totally." True.

"Then set your priorities right. You have more dating trouble than anyone I've ever seen. I love you like a daughter, but we both know you haven't had much luck picking the right men. It's time for you to use your head and find someone right."

Susan knew she'd made mistakes where men were concerned—the few she'd tried dating. They always never lasted because she had to put her work first. Building a business wasn't easy. Especially in a man's world. It caused them to think she was bossy. *Bossy!* That word ate at her. But it was the fact that she always picked men who couldn't appreciate her for the person she was or what she did for a living.

"I'm not falling for the guy, Betty. I didn't ask him to come back to town. I also didn't ask him to be the one who found me when I drove off the road. But as much as I hate admitting it, he was there and the situation could have been much worse. And if it had been worse he would have been someone good to be there to help me."

Betty looked apologetic. "I know, honey. I can't argue that he's not a good man—my goodness, look what he does for a livin'. But he just isn't the right one for you. You know I worry about you."

"Betty, I have this under control." She glanced at the clock and knew if she was going to break the contracting news she needed to do it soon. "Actually, I need to tell you something before appointments start rolling in."

"Why is it I suddenly get the idea I ain't gonna like what you've got to say?"

Susan cleared her throat. "I don't think you are. But it couldn't be helped or, believe me, I would have done something different."

Betty's green eyes narrowed.

Susan gulped—*she never gulped!* "I hired him to take over the construction on the clinic."

Betty whacked the appointment book. "Well, if that just don't beat all. What were you thinking?"

"Well, I needed someone and he was available." Susan's temper flared. What else did Betty expect her to do?

"That may be so. But you better be on guard is all I've got to say. I've said my piece." She clamped her mouth shut for five seconds. "And further more, if you think I'm gonna *smile* and make nice when I know what he's up to—well," she harrumphed. "Then you better just tell Mr. Cole Turner he don't need to be comin' around here, 'cause I'll put a finger in his chest and back him up to that there door so fast he'll think a herd of bulls done ran slap over him!"

What did she think Cole was up to anyway? The man was simply helping her out of a hard situation…*and now you're taking up for the man?* "Betty, really, you are overreacting." She was relieved to see a truck drive up. "It looks like the day is about to begin."

Betty grinned as she picked up her pencil and plopped into her chair behind the reception desk. "And ain't that just lucky for you. I'll shut up now."

"Oh, but I'm certain it'll only be for a few minutes." Susan laughed and headed toward her office, still confused about what exactly Betty thought Cole was up to.

Behind her Betty's grumble was loud and clear. "You got that right."

"So is Wyatt coming to town or what?" Cole asked his brother as he buttered biscuits. He'd squeezed in some time with Seth and his new sister-in-law before heading over to get things rolling at his new job—the job he was still a little startled to have.

"Your guess is as good as mine," Seth said as he set a plate of sausage and bacon on the table while Melody finished dishing up the scrambled eggs at the stove. "Didn't he tell you it would be Wednesday or Thursday?"

"Yeah, but I'll believe it when I see it."

"Oh, I hope he does," Melody said. "Seth, did you know he was supposed to be coming home?"

Seth nodded at her and Cole caught the glimmer of love in his brother's eyes as they connected with his new wife's. Cole really was happy for them. His heart still tugged every time he looked at them, but it was a good tug. Wyatt had been wrong when he'd thought he wasn't happy for them.

Bittersweet at what he was missing, yes, but overjoyed that God had put them together. God and *Wyatt.* It was still strange every time he thought of his big brother setting them up.

Seth started refilling their coffee mugs. "You know how Wyatt likes to run the show. He sounded to me like he had a motive for wanting you back in town, Cole. Any ideas?"

Cole's head jerked up at the question. He wasn't going to tell them that Wyatt was holding his unresolved issues of losing Lori and *their* happy-ever-after over his head. "I think he wanted me home so I'd get to know my new sister-in-law better. I sort of skipped out on y'all early after the wedding…not that the two of you were noticing anything but each other."

"I have to agree with you," Seth said, setting the coffee carafe back on the burner. "I barely noticed you'd left. Sorry, brother."

"Seth, that's horrible!" Melody looked up sheepishly as Seth dropped a kiss on her cheek. "But," she squeaked, "it is true. I was so happy to be Mrs. Seth Turner that all I could think about was Seth. We really are glad you came home, though."

Cole liked Melody. She was sweet and kind and perfect for Seth. "I am, too," he said, and meant it. That wasn't so a week ago. He thought about that as he carried the biscuits to the table. What had changed?

Seth said the blessing a few moments later and Cole felt a peace in the room as the prayer ended and they tucked in. He'd been working so hard and running, as his brothers knew he was, from the past but Cole was happy for Seth and Melody. It was a precious thing—the joy he saw in their eyes.

"So," Seth said after food was dished up and they'd started to munch on bacon and eggs, "I'm still surprised you took on Susan's remodel. But it's a good thing."

"I know she'll appreciate it," Melody said. "She's about run ragged. We've all been so happy that she decided to do this especially after her falling asleep at the wheel."

"Stubborn woman," he grunted before taking a chunk out of a biscuit.

"She is," Seth said. "But good as gold and driven. She told me once that she was the success she was because her daddy raised her up to stand on her own two feet. She hasn't said much but his death hit her hard."

Cole let that sink in. She'd lost someone she loved. "She's a tough one, that's for sure. I can see where a dad raised her. What about her mom?" Okay, so he was curious.

"Susan doesn't talk about her. But once she mentioned that she didn't remember her."

Melody sighed. "I'm hoping she finds a good man. Someone who'll love her like she deserves and fill the empty holes I believe she fills with her work… I used to do that," she said, reaching out for Seth's hand. "And then I met you."

Cole took a swig of coffee and tried to ignore the way those words made him feel.

It seemed he and Susan had more than a few things in common.

Chapter Eight

The sun was high in the April afternoon sky as Cole climbed from his truck and headed inside the clinic. From the cattle pens around the back of the building he could hear the low bawl of a few cattle and from inside the clinic, the hectic bark of dogs.

He opened the door—he'd expected from what she'd told him that it would be busy… he hadn't expected chaos!

"Get that dog back—" a pint-size woman yelled from behind the counter as she waved a magazine at a huge shaggy beast of a dog. The owner of the animal was straining to hold the leash while another woman was trying to coax a hissing cat down from the shelf behind the angry woman.

The dog barked like the echoing of a

cannon as Cole closed the door behind him. Cole had made some bad choices in life, but in that instant, walking into the fray had to be at the top of the list. The terrified cat sprang toward him claws out and hit Cole square in the chest—it did *not* feel good.

"Hold him!" *all* the women screamed—as if he needed to hold on to a cat using him as a scratching post. Thankfully, one second the yellow tabby was hooked into his chest and the next it flew to the floor and under a magazine table.

The overexcited woofer spun. Magazines exploded everywhere as the dog hit the small brown table like a linebacker.

Cole hadn't moved, too stunned by what he'd walked into to move. This was *crazy,* he thought, lunging for the leash in an attempt to save the cat.

But before he could help the cornered tabby it took charge, reared up and with a terrifying hiss, slapped the bully across the nose.

Three wide-eyed women flattened against their chair backs clutching their trembling pooches as a new battle threatened.

Cole stormed across the room, snagged the leash and yanked the dog back just as the fed-up cat launched toward it—

Cole's timing couldn't have been worse.

He stepped straight into the line of attack as the cat overshot the dog! Cole had turned back into a human scratching post when Susan rushed out of nowhere and threw a sheet over the cat.

Startled, the terrified cat let go of his arm and Cole watched in shock as Susan disappeared into another room with the secured animal.

The room went silent.

Everyone—including the dog at his side—seemed to be holding their breaths.

"I don't know who you are," the pint-sized woman said, breaking the silence. "But, oh, boy, am I glad to see you."

"Not sure I'm glad to be here," he growled about the time Susan came striding back into the room—*without* the cat.

"Betty, please take Sampson into exam room two. You," she barked the command to Cole. "Come with me, you're bleeding."

He had never been happier to be bossed around in all of his life.

He gladly turned over the leash to Betty then followed Susan into the exam room.

Oh, yeah, he was bleeding all right. He left a trail as he went.

"What *was* that?" he asked, as she pushed him to sit on the edge of the small animal exam table.

"I'm not exactly sure. Sampson is just a big puppy and normally a doll. But I'd just given him his shots and he was a little shaken up, I gue—" She stopped speaking and was staring at Cole's arm in horror. "I'm so sorry you got caught up in it."

"It's okay." He didn't want to make her feel any worse. She shook her head and reached for his shredded shirtsleeve. A quick and gentle roll exposed a not-so-pretty sight.

"I'm not even going to ask if that hurts— I know exactly how it feels." She leaned closer, her fingers trailing along his arm as she cataloged his injuries. "It doesn't look like you'll need stitches." She looked up and met his gaze.

"I'm sure you've been attacked many times in this line of business," he said, feeling no pain, only her gentle touch.

She batted her Mediterranean blues at him and for a moment he was lost in them.

She suddenly backed up, spun away and began washing her hands at the sink as if realizing she'd forgotten to sanitize before touching him. "It's a job risk," she said briskly. "I seem to keep involving you in all my job risks."

"True. Maybe we should stop meeting this way."

She gave a tiny smile, more grimace than anything. "I agree. No more mishaps from this day forward. Mine or yours."

He grinned at her as she began cleaning the punctures.

"Do you often have to deal with that sort of craziness?"

She shook her head. "Betty usually foresees disaster before it happens. She orchestrates the waiting room and exam perfectly. But today..." She frowned. "Her timing was off."

Maybe not, Cole thought, watching her work. He would have missed the feel of her touch otherwise as she gently put antiseptic on the wounds. As crazy as it sounded, the sting of alcohol had never been more welcome. Her blond hair was in its usual ponytail, falling over her shoulder as she worked. She lifted serious eyes to his.

"This may get infected."

"I work disasters, Doc. It'll be fine. I've been attacked by scared animals before."

"Really?" Her eyes widened. "I hadn't thought of that."

He shrugged. "You name it, I've most likely tangled with it."

She started to wrap a bandage around the worst wound. "Did you get some sleep last night?" he asked.

She stepped away from him. "Yes, I did. That's two nights in a row. It was wonderful. I may not be so lucky tonight."

"Let's hope the emergency night calls hold off until I get your clinic done. Speaking of which. I stopped by to tell you that I've picked up enough Sheetrock and supplies to get started tonight. By the time I get back to Mule Hollow this afternoon the demolition should be complete."

"You're kidding?"

"Hey, don't look so startled. I told you I knew what I was doing."

"Yes, I know. I guess I wasn't expecting you to jump in the very next morning."

"Why not?"

"Where did you find the help so quickly?"

He liked surprising her. The thought hit him that he liked seeing the light it brought to her eyes. And the touch of a flush it put in her cheeks. "You *see,*" he drawled, "that's where it comes in handy to have hired hands already working at the ranch. Cowboys are some of the best jacks-of-all-trades you can find."

She crossed her arms and leaned her hip against the counter. "Yes, they are. But still I didn't expect anyone to have the time."

"Seth helped out on that end by making the time for them. He's managing for a few days." He didn't need to tell her that it was a tough time to be loaning out help. Susan knew the business. "The whole town wants their favorite doctor safe."

He half expected her to bridle at the mere insinuation that she might not be safe. She didn't, though—must have been because he was injured.

"I'm ready to be there, too. You look like that shocks you."

"I'm just startled that you didn't jump on me for suggesting that you couldn't handle the drive and the work."

She smiled, her lips turning up just enough that she looked apologetic. "Speaking of work. I hate this happened to you, but I need to get to my appointments before they pile up so far back we have all kinds of cat and dog fights in the waiting room. Are you sure you're okay?"

"I'm good as new, Doc." He hopped from

the exam table and rolled his tattered sleeve down. "It's out *there* that worries me." He yanked his head toward the door and grinned. "Who knows what waits on the other side of that door."

"Oh, I promise I'll get you out of here without any more damage to your body. You just stick with me," she teased, moving to go out ahead of him.

"I'm feeling good about my chances with you in the lead. Hey, I almost forgot. I came by to ask about some wall placements." She leaned against the door and listened as he quickly explained a couple of minor changes to what they'd talked about the day before. Hearing she liked his idea, he felt satisfaction knowing she appreciated an improvement and recognized it as such.

She made the move to open the door. He touched her arm, drawing her attention. "When do you think you'll get to come out?"

"Um." Her brows crinkled. "It will be tonight after work if I can catch up—which I will, if the rest of the day goes without mishap."

"Then, I'll be there. If for some reason I miss you, you know, like if Seth needs me at the ranch or something like that, then call this number and I'll meet you there." He tugged his billfold from his back pocket and withdrew a business card. "Hopefully, we will both have uneventful afternoons."

She opened the door and he walked out into the reception room, which was in perfect order. The pint-size woman hurried from around the counter.

"Thanks again for saving the day. Dad-blame horse of a dog had a bee in its bonnet after Susan stuck that needle in him. I'm Betty, by the way."

Cole took the hand she offered him and shook. "Glad to meet you, Betty. I'm Cole Turner." No sooner was his name out of his mouth than Betty's mouth clamped tight and her eyes beaded.

She shot Susan a weird little look that he was certain had some kind of hidden message in it.

He lifted a brow and hitched a half grin. "Is something wrong?"

"Oh, *yeah,* Buster Brown. You planning to hit the road again after you get that building done?"

"Betty!"

Cole not only heard the warning in Susan's tone, but saw it in her eyes. What was going on here? It was clear that Betty was none too pleased with him. "Most likely. Is something wrong here?"

"No. Everything is just fine." Susan glared at her receptionist.

"It is not," Betty huffed.

Cole chuckled. Tiny Betty was like a miniature hen protecting her chick. What was up with her? Did she think he was here to play around—

"Someone needs to put all the cards out on the table. He needs to know I won't tolerate him—"

"Betty, please. Clients," Susan said under her breath as she took Betty by the shoulders and hustled her toward one of the exam rooms. "I need you to go and check on Tabby and make sure that he's calmed down after that scare he had."

"He is—but—"

"Go, Betty. I mean it." Susan opened the door and practically pushed Betty through the opening. Before she disappeared, Betty got in another glare at him that said this conversation would be continued.

Susan swung around and leaned against the closed door. "Sorry. Betty tends to get riled up easy."

"You don't say? What was she—"

Susan blushed…a full rose-pink. Not the pink cheeks like he'd seen before but an all-out hairline-to-neckline color change. And then he got it. "Ohhhh, she thinks—"

"I really have to get back to work." Susan glanced self-consciously about the packed waiting room and the women who'd all seemed to lean forward in their seats. Cole laughed, knowing that Susan was trying to stomp out a fire that was already well out of control.

She was definitely the talk of the town—or towns, since this was Ranger and there was no doubt in his mind that the same specu-lation was happening in Mule Hollow.

He grinned at her and she did not take it well. Oh, no, she snapped a hand to his good arm, yanked open the front door and shoved him outside.

"I'll see you tonight," she hissed, then pulled the door closed in his face.

Cole couldn't help laughing. Small-town life…he chuckled halfway home thinking about the look of horror on Susan's face. There was one thing for certain and that was Susan wasn't lovin' life in a small town right now.

Chapter Nine

"Wow!" Susan exclaimed when she walked through the front door around seven that evening.

Cole pulled the trigger of the nail gun, shooting the last nail into place on the wall he'd just studded in. "It looks different, doesn't it?" He studied her, having wondered how she would act when she arrived. She had composed herself, it seemed, since there was no pink in sight. He missed it instantly.

"Are you kidding me? This is unbelievable. You're practically ready to install Sheetrock." She was clearly amazed. "How fast do you work?"

He glanced at the progress, unimpressed. "It's not that big a deal. Do you know how easy it is to tear stuff out when two men have sledgehammers and Sawzalls? By the time I got back to town the fellas had things cleared out and the place swept. All I had to do was start cutting and nailing. Piece of cake."

"To *you* maybe. I wouldn't have known the first place to start."

"And I'm quite sure that your animal clients would rather you know how to set a bone rather than how to set concrete or use a reciprocating saw. Sampson would have eatin' all of us if I'd been the one who gave him a shot." He held up the nail gun, pretending it was a needle.

Susan laughed. "You're right. Please don't remind me. How are your wounds?"

He shrugged. "I'll live." He started to ask how Betty was but decided she wouldn't find the subject funny. He'd been thinking about that blush that had overcome her after what Betty had insinuated. An antimatchmaker... Smart woman that Betty.

Still, he'd been thinking about Susan off and on all afternoon. That blush showed the softer side of the doctor. He wondered if she showed that side of herself to anyone— freely. Today it had been forced.

"You want to help?" he asked, deciding to steer away from what he knew she was embarrassed about. After all, she'd slammed the door on him. He hid his grin. "I mean, you don't need to. I have it under control. But anytime you want to learn a little about the construction business you just let me know. I'm your man." He was teasing her, but she bristled.

"I don't think that'll be necessary," she said primly. "I have plenty on my plate." No way was she helping him.

"Susan, relax. I was just teasing. I wasn't really expecting you to learn construction."

"Right. I knew that. I— Well, it's been a frantic day and I'm still a little keyed up," she said with an embarrassed laugh. "I actually do know how to use a hammer. My dad made sure of that."

"Well, that's a good thing," he mused, enjoying watching her. The fact that they were alone in a big room that suddenly seemed to shrink about them had his attention.

She looked away and it hit him that they'd been staring at each other for a lengthy moment. He plopped his boot to the concrete—*back to work*. "Let me show you what will be happening tomorrow." He grabbed the plans and rolled them out on the plywood board set across two sawhorses. "You can change anything you don't like now, but if you want the job finished quickly, I'd hold off on changing things as I'm working."

She moved to stand beside him and studied the pages. He couldn't help taking a deep breath—she'd obviously showered before she'd driven to town and she smelled of soap; it was as appealing as the clean crisp air of a new spring morning. Nothing floral or too sweet for Susan; this scent fit her. He forced his attention to the plans, wishing she'd smelled of dogs, horses and antiseptic…only problem was he didn't think even that would have taken away from the way she had his attention.

"These are the walls we talked about and the changes we discussed this morning." Whipping the pencil from behind his ear, he pointed to the prints he'd drawn. "On these four walls I added a few more plugs for you. No one can ever have enough."

"You're right about that." She leaned forward and studied the page. Tucking her loose hair behind her ear exposed her profile more clearly. Again, there was nothing about Susan Worth that resembled old Doc

Crampton—the crotchety old man who had been the veterinarian in this area for as long as Cole could remember. When he'd been a kid, Cole had thought Doc Crampton was a hundred years old. But Doc had only just retired a few years ago…. Nope, Susan didn't look like the vets he was used to seeing. And he liked it—matter of fact, if he lived in Mule Hollow he'd be tempted to manufacture emergencies just so she would be at the ranch as much as possible.

"It looks just like what I explained to you," she said. Turning her head to face him, she caught him staring. "I like it."

He liked her. The knowledge hit him like a hundred-mile-an-hour wind gust. As if feeling the same blast, Susan inhaled sharply, gave him a tart nod and stepped away.

There was chemistry here.

Wide-open attraction…and he was enjoying it. He grinned at the idea. Not Susan, though. Oh, no, the good doctor's eyes narrowed, making him want to grin bigger. He didn't.

"I think you have everything under control," she said. "I'll leave you to it, then, so you can get home at a decent hour." She glanced at her watch as if to underscore her words.

"That sounds good," Cole said. Dropping his pencil on the plans, he removed his tool belt, still holding her gaze as she backed toward the door. "This is a pretty good time to call it a night."

"Oh. Okay," she snapped, turned and strode quickly out the door.

Ran was a better word for how fast she exited. He followed her, pausing to set the lock and pull the door shut behind him. "I thought I'd head to Sam's for a bite to eat. Want to join me?"

She stopped with her hand resting on her car door handle. "I don't think that would be a good idea."

"And why is that?" he asked. He'd expected her to turn him down but hadn't expected it to be so disappointing. "You have to eat. I have to eat," he pressed—crazy as it was, he did it anyway.

Crazier still was her hesitation. "This is true…but I just think you and me together, dining in public, isn't a good combination. This—" she waved her hand toward the clinic "—this is a business association. Nothing more."

He held his expression blank when he'd

felt like hiking a brow at her tone. He got her message loud and clear. A message he found a little insulting, truth be told. "Sorry I stepped over that line. You have a nice evening, boss."

He stalked to his truck. Sure it was a business relationship. It wasn't as if *he* was the one trying to do all this matchmaking. He wasn't even interested that way. Sure there was chemistry there—big-time. But so what? He was doing this job and hitting the road. She and Betty didn't need to be all up in arms thinking he believed in any of the town's nonsense.

He climbed into his truck. Susan hadn't moved. She was glaring at him from the same spot she'd been standing in as he walked away. Oh, she was hot at him for walking away—he'd given her what she wanted and now she looked insulted. He tipped his cap to her, then turned the key and revved the engine like a sixteen-year-old.

What a horrible day! Make that a horrible week. She watched Cole's truck disappear down the road and wondered—as she'd been wondering ever since she hired him—about her sanity.

Betty had been right on with her concern. Susan wasn't sure how her receptionist had zeroed in on Susan's attraction to Cole and the flaws inherent in that but she had…even before Susan had taken a bite of a doughnut that morning.

Not that Susan needed to be told she'd be alone with an aching heart if she let herself act on her feelings.

Feelings. They were something that needed to be controlled. Her daddy had taught her to work, achieve her goals and not let feelings get in the way of those goals. Especially feelings for men. She figured out as she'd gotten older that part of that stemmed from the fact that he wanted to spare her the pain of losing someone she loved…but she'd learned after his death that that pain couldn't be avoided. Still, she'd hardly dated all the way through college. She'd worked so hard to make her daddy proud. He hadn't been there to push her, but his memory had and continued to give her the spur she needed.

She blinked against the emotion that welled up and threatened suddenly to overflow. She sniffed and brushed a tear off her cheek. She didn't cry much. What good did it do? Certainly none to cry over Cole Turner.

She swiped her fingers across her cheek, catching a lone tear as she stared at her new clinic. She should be happy. This was a great day. A turning point in her life. She'd been alone since her dad's death. But this was going to change that. She just needed to stop thinking about Cole.

And she *was* thinking about him. Ever since hiring him she'd fretted that she'd made a major mistake. Today had confirmed that on all counts. There was a chemistry between them that she couldn't deny when she'd tended the wounds Tabby had inflicted on him. Especially every time she touched his arm. Feelings. It was only feelings. Taking the advice of her dad—as always—she knew she couldn't let her emotions lead her where Cole was concerned. She was looking for a forever cowboy. A cowboy who'd be there for her and help her in her business. Someone who would think she was worth loving and sticking around for…a man who would not only be there for her but also for their children.

Nope. Susan was moving to Mule Hollow to find a cowboy she could love…not one who loved the road.

* * *

Cole walked out onto the porch of the stagecoach house. The night air was cool and heavy with the scent of honeysuckle and he inhaled, hoping it would calm his restless spirit. Churning thoughts had finally driven him from bed and out into the night.

He'd dressed in jeans and boots and decided to take advantage of the moonlit night, see if it helped him.

He'd stopped having sleepless nights over Lori some time ago. Six years was a long time. He missed her and regretted every day of the life they'd not had the chance to have, but he'd stopped waking up over it during the second year. It had just happened, as if his subconscious had accepted that some things couldn't be changed.

God did make some dreams come true. Some people's.

In his job he got to help rebuild lost dreams.

It was a satisfying endeavor.

He'd come to enjoy it and it helped ease his discontentment. Tonight, he'd awakened with Susan on his mind and he had stirred that discontent inside of him ten-fold.

He didn't really know her. All he knew about her was that she was a hard worker, stubborn and well respected. She was also beautiful, but he'd been around many, many women since Lori and none of them had cracked the wall he'd built around himself.

"You're not looking for Susan to crack it, either," he reminded himself.

He would be heading back to the coast as soon as he finished this job for her. And when he finished doing his work there he'd move on to the next town that had fallen victim to a natural disaster.

He'd only taken this job of Susan's because she needed him—why he took all of his jobs, really. He had the ability to fix someone's problems where his hands and backbone were concerned. It was something he was driven to do. It was something he wouldn't give up.

He'd always liked to travel. He'd dreamed of seeing the world through a cowboy's eyes…it had been his dream. But dreams changed. His had changed when he'd met Lori.

Her sweet face hovered in the back of his memory like the delicate flower of a woman she'd been. Pressing it aside, he concentrated on the sound of his boot steps as they clicked along the stone sidewalk. It led to the aged stone wall at the back of the stagecoach house. Needing the distraction, he let his mind wander. The stone wall had probably been built at the same time the house itself was built. The fireplace running up the side of the house was built from the same stone, so it was a good indicator. He liked that the low-slung wall with its iron gate was built in the early 1800s, too. He loved the family history of this place, the lasting power it represented, too. The hinges creaked as he opened the gate, the noise almost lost in the sound of the rushing river. The moonlight sparkled off the twenty-six stone steps that led down to the rocky river edge. It was a great place to think. He'd come here often growing up.

Mostly he'd come here to dream of seeing the world—of leaving.

Tonight he came because a tall blonde wouldn't get off his mind. Susan had drifted into his dreams and thoughts of her wouldn't be denied.

He tucked his hands in his pockets and wished his agitated musings could be tucked away as easily. Not so.

Susan had dreams. She'd worked hard for them and from what he could tell she didn't know when to say no. She didn't have a balance in her life. For her own good, she needed balance.

He could help there. God had brought him home at the right time to help her. When he finished her clinic, living there would help her be safer, hopefully more rested. Then again, if she was moving to town to find a husband, that'd mean she was going to date. And dating might take up more time than the driving she'd done between Mule Hollow and Ranger.

Unwanted, the idea of her dating sat in his gut like a sour lump of milk. He shifted his weight from one boot to the other and frowned. The doc might be planning to date, but she was keeping *their* relationship on a business level. He raked both hands through his hair as he stared up at the sky.

Bone-deep loneliness settled into him. He'd coped with the loneliness over the years by focusing his energies on his work. Things had been fine. Thoughts of Lori had driven away any desire to look for female companionship. He was young—his buddies hadn't been able to understand how he "stayed out of the game" as they'd called it. But it had been easier than they could ever know.

Ask her out again. There they were again: the words that had driven him from his bed. They rumbled through his thoughts and his lonely heart ached.

Chapter Ten

"So what do you think about this color?" Lacy asked on Saturday morning as she stepped back from the wall she'd just painted green. Holding her paintbrush in one hand she propped it on her jutting hip while she waved her other pink-tipped hand toward the wall. "It looks like green apples to me. Not that I don't *love* me some green apples, but this is a small room. As weird as it is for me to admit it, all this loudness might run you crazy."

She was right—but Susan was so shocked to hear that *Lacy* was actually thinking the bright color was too much. Lacy never backed down from color—why, her hair salon was pinker than her fingernails! The woman had talked a bunch of down-home cowboys into painting Mule Hollow every color God had ever created. But now, standing here in the tiny living room of what was about to become Susan's home, the irrepressible blonde bombshell was questioning the brightness of a relatively mild color. It was a bit confusing—kind of like Susan's life in general right now…with work, moving and Cole. Thoughts of the man had complicated her life all week—but she wasn't dwelling on that today.

"Are you sure you feel all right?" she asked, focusing on what was going on right now.

"Yeah," Molly Jacobs gasped through the open window of the porch. She was confined to outdoors painting because she was pregnant. Mule Hollow was having a run on pregnant women. Several were expecting and many were thinking about it. Before long the population was going to explode. That would make the matchmakers happy, since it would mean their original idea to bring women to town to marry the lonesome cowboys was an all-star success.

Molly was the local syndicated newspaper reporter who'd been here from almost the moment Lacy and her friend Sheri had driven into town in Lacy's 1958 pink Cadillac convertible. The matchmakers had the original dream and Lacy had come to town, bringing spunk and momentum to the plan.

But Molly had taken the plan to the next level when she'd joined in on the campaign. She'd come to town to do an article for her Houston newspaper about the wacky little town. She'd ended up staying on and creating a weekly column that people across the nation had begun to follow. The exposure still brought women to the tiny growing town.

The story fascinated Susan even after three years and all she could hope was that one of these days one of the cowboys would be hers.

Cole Turner's face appeared in her mind's eye like a thorn digging in. It had been a week since she'd told him she didn't want to have anything but a working relationship between them. He'd been overly careful at every meeting since to keep it just that.

So much so that it was beginning to irritate her.

Why exactly was that?

And why was she so scared to have dinner with him? She knew the facts—that he was leaving. So why not enjoy dinner and let it go at that? She was an adult, after all.

Because that was just the way it needed to be. The safe way.

Pulling her head out of the clouds, Susan focused on the candy-apple-green swiped across her living-room wall.

"Seriously," she said. "Why is this tone wrong for me? I might like bright colors, too. Or are you saying I'm too boring?"

Lacy rolled her baby blues at the teasing comment. "You know I like to be unpredictable," Lacy said. "But, Susan, face it, you're more reserved than me—this green paint *might* just make you crazy."

From the porch, Molly's hoot of laughter broke Lacy off and covered up Susan's own chuckle. "We all know a *lot, lot, lot* more reserved would be the accurate wording."

Molly stuck her head back in the window. "But then everyone is a lot more reserved than Lacy! Hey, heads up, the cavalry is arriving."

Molly had barely gotten the words out before the sound of numerous vehicles could be heard heading up the drive. Susan shot Lacy a startled look. "What's going on?"

Lacy grinned. "Surely you didn't think we were going to do all the work, just the three and a half of us? I got here early to butter you up. Molly's been slacking off on the painting to take notes for her column, as always!"

Molly wagged her tiny pocket notebook through the window.

"I should have known," Susan groaned as Lacy took her by the arm and led her toward the door. Unexpected tears welled in her eyes at the sight of the smiling folks hopping from their trucks and cars.

Mule Hollow might have started out with only the matchmakers, who were striding her way, but it now had a wonderful group of gals calling it home. And they were here to help and welcome her. Susan suddenly felt overwhelmingly blessed. God was good. Losing her father had been so hard but this felt so right…like she was at last making a home.

Haley Bell Sutton, the local real estate agent who'd sold Susan this place, came up the steps, her curly blond hair bouncing. She handed Susan a frilly bag. "Happy housewarming." She engulfed Susan in a hug. "I'm here to paint, but you know what a klutz I am, so you might want to keep me outside with the babies or something."

"You are not a klutz. Thank you so much for coming."

Before she could say more, Rose Cantrell came sweeping up the steps. "We're so happy you've finally decided to join us as an actual resident." She hugged her and held up another bright package. "I'll start a stack over here by Molly so you won't have to try to juggle them all."

A truck bounced to a stop and Tacy Jones hopped out. "Whoo-hoo—thought I was gonna be late!" She jogged up the steps with a red package tied with a red bandana. She was a cowgirl through and through, even down to her gift wrap. "Are we glad to have you here! Birdy and her new pack of pups send you their love."

Susan chuckled as Tacy hugged her. Birdy was Tacy's excellent blue heeler and she'd recently had some beautiful, healthy puppies that buyers were anxiously waiting to take home with them. "Speaking of Birdy and her crew, I'll be out first of next week to give them their last checkup before they go to their new homes."

"Roger that," Tacy said as Esther Mae stepped up. She, Norma Sue and Adela had been unloading refreshments from their truck with the help of Lacy and Molly.

"I'm getting me a new dog, Susan," she punctuated her announcement with a bear hug. "Thought I'd better get you ready. Me and my Hank are heading over to pick her up tomorrow."

"Great. I'll be glad to see her—"

"Tell her what kind," Norma Sue broke in, shaking her wiry halo of gray curls. "It's the dumbest thing I ever heard of."

"Now, Norma," Adela called from where she was slicing a cake. "Don't start." Her bright blue eyes sparkled with teasing.

Esther Mae's grin widened. "A Dorky!"

"A what?" The question rippled about the group that was growing by the carload.

"A Dorky," Norma Sue said, loud and clear. "One good thing about it, the name fits Esther," Norma Sue chuckled the last words.

"A Dorky," Susan said. "I've seen the little dogs and they're cute as can be—dorky-looking but cute."

"What are they?" Haley asked.

Esther Mae patted the edge of her hairdo with pride. "A cross between a dachshund and a Yorkshire terrier. You know, a Yorkie. They call the little darlings Dorkies. You should see my baby." She cooed the last sentence. "I'll get her tomorrow. She's just a teacup of fur right now. Some of them are straight-haired but my Toot is curls, curls and more curls."

"What made you decide to get a puppy?" Susan asked.

"Well, with all these new babies being born I just thought a cute little puppy to play with would be fun for them. You know me, it's all about the brownie points and I want these babies to love their grandma Esther best."

"Ha! We'll see about that," Norma Sue huffed.

Adela came over and slipped an arm around Susan's waist. "Let's get this housework started and get Susan ready to move in. Norma Sue and Esther Mae can fight over their grandma status any time," she said.

As always, when Miss Adela spoke, everyone listened. She was the tiny, soft-spoken one but she was the leader when all was said and done. She always, always led by example and Susan wished she could be half the woman Adela was. She was a strong woman of faith. As were most of the women she knew who lived in Mule Hollow. They all just lived their faith in different ways. Lacy was an all-out in-your-face believer compared to Adela's quiet, steady faith—both were joyful. The idea hit Susan out of the blue. Her faith was more plodding. Did she have joy in her faith?

Why was she asking herself this? Her life was great. What she didn't like about it, she was changing. In the midst of the time she was supposed to be happiest, she was suddenly questioning things about herself that she'd never ever thought about before.

But now the group of women had reached critical mass and Susan was swept into a welcoming party she hadn't anticipated.

The gifts and food were wonderful. However, the sweetest thing of all was that everyone came dressed to work.

"Thank y'all for coming," she said. "My daddy always said that a true friend was the one who showed up to do the work." That got a big laugh, but looking around the porch full of smiling women, she felt extremely happy.

Despite her questions, her future seemed awfully bright. As she stood there, the sound of a saw slicing through wood drifted from the clinic building…Cole.

She was suddenly overcome with the insane notion to walk over there and ask him if he wanted to go out to dinner sometime.

Maybe Lacy was right. Maybe the apple-green paint was making her crazy after all.

Cole stretched the measuring tape out on the two-by-four then glanced up at the sound of another car headed toward Susan's house.

Something was going on—it looked like a meeting of the entire town of women. He was marking his measurement when a truck pulled up outside and stopped.

A few minutes later Seth stepped through the doorway.

"It's about time you showed up," he said, finishing his mark.

"Don't you be giving free labor a hard time," Seth grunted. "I had to tend to my own business before I came down here to offer my services."

"Yeah, yeah, stop with the sob story," Cole said, heading over to start framing another wall in. He and his brothers loved to give each other a hard time. He and Wyatt especially enjoyed needling Seth, since he'd always tended to be the serious one. Of course, Cole had been a whole lot more serious since falling in love with Lori and watching her die. Watching someone fight that hard to survive changed the way a person viewed life.

Then again, it also made a person grateful for family, and his brothers had stood by him even in the darkest moments. Even when they hadn't known how dark his days had gotten. He'd sent his horse home and bought his Harley the same day they'd laid Lori to rest in the tiny cemetery outside her hometown in Colorado. He'd hit the road unsure of where he was going or what he was doing. All he'd known was he had to go. His brothers had been worried, but they'd stood back and let him do his thing while making sure he knew they were there for him when he needed them. It had been his cousin Chance who had set him on the course of working the disaster areas. Chance was a rodeo preacher and he'd been helping rebuild some of the thousands of miles of fences that had been wiped out by Hurricane Rita. He'd encouraged Cole during a brief phone call to come help with the devastation. He'd started with Rita, and when Ike had hit the coast two years ago, he'd continued to do what he'd been doing. It was odd how disaster had been a blessing to him when he'd needed something to pour his grief into. God had put Chance where he needed to be.

He could see it now.

"Any idea what's going on up at the house?" he asked.

Seth grabbed a board and handed it to him. "They're having a housewarming and paint party. Melody's over there."

"I must have missed her as she drove by."

"So how are things going between you and Susan?"

"Nowhere for things to be going."

They worked in silence for a few minutes, then Seth stopped fitting a board into place. "Cole, what's going on inside your head these days? Aren't you getting the least little bit ready to settle down?"

Cole shot a nail into the board then leaned back on his haunches to stare up at his brother. "Honestly, I think about it every now and again. Lately it's been there."

Seth's lip twitched upward on one side. "I was hoping you might. Seriously, Cole. I'm starting to need some more help on this end, not to put pressure on you or Wyatt. I've been happy to run this ranch, but since we bought the other ranch, it's taking up more time than I'm wanting to give. I'm married now."

Cole stood. "Why haven't you said anything about this before?"

"I've talked with Wyatt about it."

"But not me."

Seth lifted a shoulder. "I'm talking to you now."

Cole knew Seth like a book. His brother wouldn't say anything unless he meant it. "So what exactly are you saying?"

"I'm saying it's time for you to come home. It's time for you to put your past behind you."

Cole was caught off guard. "What if I don't want to?"

Seth locked eyes with him. "It's time."

There was more in those two words than business. This was about more than ranching and Cole knew it. "You'd force me to come home?"

Seth laughed a harsh laugh. "You know me better than that. All I have to do is hire a manager from yours and Wyatt's profits and that'd solve the problem right there…which was Wyatt's second suggestion."

"But I was his first suggestion?"

"Bingo. I didn't think you were ready, but I went along with him getting you back here. Now I believe it is time. Wyatt is right."

"Wait…you went along with it?" That got Cole's attention. "Do you know how he got me back here?"

"Some crazy story about me and Melody thinking you were upset about us getting married and being happy."

"I should have known," Cole said, feeling like a fool. His big brother was always pulling stunts like this. "I didn't believe a word of it when he first started in on his tall tale. But you know how good he is at spinning tales." Wyatt was true-blue Turner. He'd inherited their great-great-great-great-grandpa Oakley's knack for spinning a tall tale. Oakley had been known to make people believe anything he said. Wyatt had the knack.

"I honestly couldn't believe you fell for it. Wyatt must have pulled out all the stops to make you believe that I would ever think you weren't happy for me."

Cole frowned. "Not as much as you think, Seth. I didn't want you to be unhappy but I'll confess it messed with my head. I left early because it just opened up old wounds. I was in a bad spot for a little while."

"Wyatt is as good at picking up on unspoken things as he is spinning tales," Seth mused. "I'm sorry you went through that and I hate that we deceived you, but honestly I agree now—it's time you came home. I need you. Forgive me. How's it going? Being here I mean?"

He knew how restless Cole got. "Strangely."

"In a good way?"

Cole set his nail gun down and scratched his jaw as he thought about how to put into words what was happening in his head. "I'm not sure. And I'm also not sure about pitching in here full-time. I hate to tell you, but as it stands you better start looking for a ranch foreman."

Chapter Eleven

The sun had gone down by the time the women of Mule Hollow packed up and called it a day. Susan still couldn't believe that every room in the small house had been painted. Her kitchen had also been scrubbed and the cabinets lined so that she was ready to unpack her things the minute she brought boxes over…of course she had yet to pack those boxes and everyone had volunteered to help with that, too.

Feeling restless, she glanced toward the clinic and saw Cole's truck was still parked outside. Taking a deep breath, she walked over. It had been an odd Saturday. For starters, she'd not scheduled any appointments so she could work on her house. Then, she'd arranged for the new vet buying her clinic in Ranger to start taking emergency calls over the next three weeks and she'd just be available for consultation during the change-over time. She'd been pleased when the vet had agreed and startled that she'd come up with the idea.

But it was the right move. Her clients there were going to have to get used to her being gone and she was going to have to let them go. She was at peace with it, though. Today she'd never thought twice about it—except to acknowledge a hopeful sense of things to come.

Cole had the large rolling bay door open leading into what had been the oil supply storage area. The door would now act as easy access for large animals and access to the holding pens that would be brought in and set up over the next couple of weeks. "Hello," she called as she entered.

"Hello, down there." Cole's head popped up over the edge of a rafter.

She laughed nervously, looking up at him. What was she doing? "What are you doing up there?"

"Running electrical wire to the new plugs. Want to come up?"

"Sure." Susan walked to the ladder propped

against an exposed steel beam. When she reached the plywood Cole met her.

"It's secured, so it's safe," he said, taking her elbow.

She stepped onto the board. "Thanks."

"Don't want anything happening to the boss." He let go of her arm instantly and went back to the coil of electrical wire he'd begun rolling across the ceiling.

"So it's looking good," she said, trying to ignore the boss comment—after all, she'd been the one to get it started.

"Thanks. It's coming along. I'll have the new paneling up on all the walls next week, and then I'll build the counters and that front area will be good to go. It'll take me the last week to get this area finished out—"

"Do you want to go to dinner?" She forced the words out before she could back out of it.

He cocked his head to the side to look up at her from his kneeling position. "Well, Doc, I'm not too sure my boss would let me off for something like that."

"Would you *stop* with the boss stuff and answer my question." She was crazy. Slap crazy!

"Since you put it that way, I guess I'd

better say yes or my boss might fire me. When?"

"How about tomorrow after church?"

He stood up. "You sure about this?"

"I asked you, didn't I?"

He laughed. "Well, yeah, you did. I'll be there."

"Good." Susan's knees were knocking and her stomach was lurching side to side so drastically she felt seasick. She'd just asked Cole on a date... "I better go," she blurted, not because she wanted to but because it was the only thing that her frazzled brain thought to say.

"How'd you manage to get off for your little shindig today?"

The question had her hesitating. He went back to work rolling out the wire. She relaxed a touch—maybe he'd just interpreted her invitation as just dinner.

"I made a deal with the new owner. He's taking over weekend emergencies in that area up until the sale date. So I took today off."

He paused and stared at her, clearly astounded. "That's good, Doc. Real good. How'd it feel having some freedom?"

His praise washed over her like warm

water and in that instant her knees stopped knocking and her stomach calmed down. She smiled—she couldn't have hidden it if she tried. "It felt great. Of course, I'm on call here in Mule Hollow."

"And amazed you didn't get any calls?"

She leaned against a steel support pole that ran from the slab below to the roof. "I am, actually. I had a couple of calls since I last saw you but other than that it's been quiet."

He'd reached a connection box. "Not my fault if that's what you're thinking."

She laughed. It had been days since she thought about how mad he'd been at Seth for getting her out to save that baby calf. "Oh, I'm glad to know you're not wasting your hard-earned cash to pay my clients not to call me."

"Don't think it didn't cross my mind the other night. You were so tired you needed someone to step in and change something."

Someone else might have thought that was a sweet thought. She didn't. "Cole, I didn't need anyone to step in and change my life. I'm quite capable of doing that myself. When *I* deemed it necessary." Here they went... right back to square one.

Her pager went off just as Cole was about to say something she was certain she wasn't going to like. This right here was the reason asking him to dinner was a ridiculous thing to do. They'd argue most of the night away.

The smug man just thought he was right about everything. It would be nice to be so perfect!

"I have to take this."

"Duty calls."

Even that irritated her. "Catch you later," she snapped and headed toward the ladder.

"Holler if you need any help," he called as she started down.

"Yeah, um, thanks." Yeah, right—like that was going to happen. Not, was more like it. Nope, she shouldn't have asked him out. He just simply took too much for granted. Her accepting help from him obviously gave him the impression that he had a right to voice his disagreement with her life. It was weird. And not something she was going to tolerate.

Cole hung his head, exasperated at himself. Why couldn't he keep his big mouth shut? He crossed to the ladder—fully intent on catching up with Susan. They'd been having a decent conversation and it had taken his mind off the things he'd been dwelling on ever since Seth dropped his bombshell that morning.

She'd thrown up the do-not-trespass sign the instant he'd said something about her lack of responsibility where her safety and well-being were concerned. Knowing her as he was beginning to think he did, she'd taken what he said as a complete slap in the face about her entire life.

The woman was hard to talk to. Skimming down the ladder, he followed her voice toward the waiting area. They'd had a phone line installed in the office on Tuesday for just such a thing as this. She was just hanging up when he walked through the door.

"Something wrong?"

"Yes. Lilly and Cort Wells—a local horse trainer—are out of town and one of their mares looks like she may be going into labor early. The young guy who is feeding for them called it in. I'm going out to make sure everything is okay."

She'd been walking toward the door while talking and Cole followed her. "You want some help?"

No way, the look she shot him over her shoulder said. "No. I'm fine."

"I might be able to help." He followed her into the night air.

She didn't give him another glance, but kept right on walking across the drive, heading toward her truck at a quick clip. He felt at loose ends as he watched her go. None of his business, though—what had he expected after what he'd said?

He'd just pulled down the large rolling door and locked up the building when she drove past. She didn't give him even a glance.

He stalked to his truck, watching her pull out of the parking lot. He should let it go. She didn't want or need his help.

As he drove onto the road, he could see her taillights in the distance. When she turned onto the main road into Mule Hollow, she went left. Cole turned right and headed the opposite direction.

He would do as she said. Mind his business and grab a chicken-fried steak at Sam's diner. Susan would be fine. She was just checking on a horse. She could do that in her sleep and there was no need to worry that she would get into any trouble out there by herself. She knew what she was doing.

Still, accidents happened.

Chapter Twelve

"Hey, Samantha, what's up?" Susan called to the mischievous donkey. Samantha ruled the roost out here at Cort and Lilly's place. They let the little donkey roam at will and had just tried to Samantha-proof the place as much as possible. "You're behaving, I hope."

Samantha batted her big brown eyes and grinned, curling her lips back, exposing a wide row of teeth. Her sidekick, Lucky, a hairy little beast with scraggly hair and whiskers, came barreling around the corner at the sound of her arrival.

Toenails scrambling for traction, he went crazy barking an enthusiastic greeting.

"How are my two favorite patients?" she asked, scratching first Samantha between the eyes, then Lucky before she headed inside to look for the mare.

Behind her she could hear Samantha's hooves prancing on the concrete as the donkey followed her. Lucky raced ahead of them barking, as if announcing her arrival to the entire barn of horses. Susan half expected all the horses to be running around free since Samantha had a habit of opening their stalls and letting them loose so she could eat their feed. Lilly had told her that she'd gotten better about that little problem since Cort had installed harder-to-open latches.

"How's our mommy-to-be?" Susan spoke soothingly as she unlatched the last stall's gate where Sweet Pea was pacing restlessly. The horse nickered and threw her head from side to side looking very unhappy. Moving inside, Susan approached her cautiously. Despite her name, Sweet Pea was pretty high-strung and Susan knew to take care.

Jake had made a good call. She was definitely in distress. She gently rubbed the mare's soft nose then ran a hand along her belly. "Not feeling so great, are you, girl? Hang in there, it's going to be okay."

Sweet Pea nudged her hard with her nose and grunted, as if to say "easy for you to say." "Believe me, I've brought plenty of colts into the world. I promise you'll be fine," she said as she examined her. When she finished she was glad to see that everything looked fine and the birth should go smoothly. Still, Susan knew to expect the unexpected.

She'd removed her rubber gloves and was tossing them through the stall gate into the trash bin Samantha was sitting beside. The donkey was on her haunches watching what was going on. Just as if she were sitting at the movies. Susan rubbed her nose before turning back when Lucky started barking—and just like that the unexpected happened....

Sweet Pea jumped, swung her hips around and slammed into Susan. Knocked off balance, Susan went down—just as Sweet Pea began to buck like a rodeo bronc.

Cole couldn't help it. He didn't like the idea of Susan being out there by herself. *Forget about it.*

Right. She didn't want him out there. Against his better judgment, he parked in front of Sam's and got out. On Saturday nights, the little town had metamorphosed into a happening place. The new theater that had opened up on the outskirts of town was partly to blame for the phenomenon. People drove into town to attend the live show and stayed around to dine at Sam's. Even during the day, the town had come alive with tourists…tourists—the very notion that his hometown now had tourists was just so weird to him. He was having to adjust to the idea. Thankfully nothing had really changed the atmosphere of Mule Hollow.

Sure, the town's clapboard buildings were now painted every color of the rainbow, but the base of the town, the good people—the roots of the place—were still the same. It was as if the town had simply spruced up a bit and become what it had dreamed of becoming. And it was drawing people to it.

When he entered the old diner, the hum of people talking and laughing almost drowned out Faith Hill singing "Mississippi Girl" on the jukebox in the corner.

There was a cute college-age gal taking an order from a large group in the far corner and through the swinging café doors leading into the kitchen he could see someone working the grill. Sam grinned at him from behind the counter.

"How goes, Cole? Coffee?"

Cole nodded. "Got you some help, I see," he said, sliding onto a stool. As long as he could remember Sam had worked the diner alone. It was a sure sign the town had grown.

"Yup. Since I'm married to Adela, I enjoy a little time off."

Cole should have guessed it. The conversation he'd had with Seth that morning shifted from the back burner of his mind to the front burner at full boil. Seth wanted more time off, too.

He wanted Cole home. Wanted him to pitch in and take responsibility beside him for the legacy they were trying hard to preserve with the ranch. Cole understood where he was coming from but it had come from left field.

"How's it goin' out thar at Susan's?" Sam said, grinning.

"It's coming along. I'm on schedule."

"That ain't what I meant and you know it. How y'all gettin' along?"

"How do you think?"

Sam chuckled. "That good, huh?"

There was a cowboy in his early twenties sitting at the counter and he tuned in to the conversation. "I just called Susan about thirty minutes ago about one of the mares out at the Wells place."

"Cole. Jake. Jake. Cole," Sam said, introducing them. "Jake here has been looking after the place."

"Nice ta meet you," Cole said, shaking hands. "She was in the office when you called."

"So did she head out there?"

"Almost before hanging up." He still wasn't happy about her being out there alone.

"That gal works too much by herself," Sam said, frowning at Cole. "Why'd you let her go out thar alone?"

"Now Sam, hold on. I offered and she shut me down."

Jake looked worried. "That mare's pretty skittish and in trouble. I'm thinkin' that foal is gonna need some help being born."

"I'll go," Cole said. "Sam, how about two of those barbecue plates to go?"

Sam's wrinkled face crinkled upward. "Sounds like a plan ta me. I'll even toss in a couple of peach cobblers."

What am I doing? "Wait. Scratch that," Cole said, thinking about how adamant Susan was. The woman was right—she was an adult who'd been on countless late-night calls. He was here only to get her building up and running. Not overtake her life.

"Scratch it?" Sam asked in disbelief.

"That's what I said. Susan'll be fine. She'll be hotter than a poker stick if I go out there. Y'all told me that from the very beginning."

"Yeah, but—" Sam scratched his head. "You sure?"

No, he wasn't sure. But what was he supposed to do? Ignore her wishes and force himself into her life whether she wanted him to or not?

Susan rolled, trying to escape Sweet Pea's hooves. She winced when one grazed her hip. Pain shot through her and she covered her head with her hands as she rolled toward the stall gate. Totally agitated out of her mind, Sweet Pea came down again. This time the blow grazed Susan's shoulder— thankfully it wasn't a full impact. Still, pain ricocheted through Susan. She cried out.

Trapped and feeling fear for the first time, Susan braced herself for the worst. Suddenly Samantha let out a loud hee-haw, the stall gate flew open and Lucky and Samantha came charging to her rescue.

Something was wrong.

The incessant barking of a dog had Cole

barreling from his truck the minute he pulled up beside Susan's truck. Tearing into the barn, he came face-to-face with the most unexpected thing he could have imagined: Samantha the donkey dragging Susan from a horse stall.

Samantha, more roll-poly than he remembered her from years ago, had a tight grip on Susan's collar and was backing out of the stall. The dog had planted its feet between Susan and the pregnant mare and was holding the frantic horse back with its yapping.

It was a circus. Racing forward, he pushed the donkey away, grabbed Susan under the arms and hauled her clear of the stall.

She was awake. Her startled eyes looked up into his as he halted in the center of the barn. She winced as he dropped to his knees and leaned her against him. "What happened? Are you hurt?"

"I got knocked over and caught under Sweet Pea's hooves. Samantha and Lucky charged to my rescue."

He touched her shoulder and the ripped shirtsleeve. "You're hurt. Where? Is this the only place?"

"It's nothing."

"Where?" he demanded.

"Just a bruised hip, shoulder and ego. That's the worst."

His temper flared. "This was just the kind of thing I was worried about happening to you." His hands tightened about her arms and he had the overwhelming urge to slide one around her and hug her tightly. "You know how fortunate you just were, don't you?" He heard the clipped edge in his voice as the strain of losing it warred within him. She could have been killed.

"Are you okay?" Cole said. His hands shook as he looked down at her. Emotions he'd locked away threatened to cave him in but he held on as Susan nodded. Their faces were close and his lips moved to her temple in a kiss before he caught himself. She stiffened in his arms and sanity flooded his mind… He swallowed and yanked back. "Good." She hadn't moved, but blinked, studying him. What was he thinking? He shot to his feet.

"Let's see if you can stand. Careful," he said, trying hard to get his focus back on being angry with her and not on the fact that he'd just kissed her temple. Barely stopping himself from giving her a real kiss.

He could have lost her.

The idea slammed into him so hard his knees went weak. She sucked in a painful breath as she leaned on his arm and rose to her feet. Immediately, she took a couple of steps away from him. He didn't move. *She's not yours to lose,* he reminded himself.

Not that way, anyway. She was not Lori.

"I'm fine," Susan said. "Nothing broken. I'll probably limp for a few days, and this arm is going to let me know it's there every time I move it, but I'm good."

Cole blinked hard. "What if you'd gotten *trampled?* What if you'd lain out here all night with no one around?" What if he hadn't listened to Sam and he'd gone on home…. His stomach twisted and he felt like throwing up. She was staring at him, stunned.

"You have no business making large-animal calls by yourself," he said, yanking the stall gate closed. Needing something, anything, to do other than to look at her.

"Don't start with me, Cole."

"Why, because you don't want to hear the truth?" He told himself to back off. Told himself this was none of his business, but this was twice he'd been there—it wasn't a coincidence. He had to get through to her. He had to make her take better care of herself. "Why are you so stubborn?"

"Because I am. Because I need to be. It's my business and my practice. I know how to handle large animals. I'm not incompetent."

They were standing toe-to-toe, both breathing hard from emotion—anger on her part. Fear and...desperation on his part. He needed to make her understand that she was precious and had a great life ahead of her. He yanked his thoughts to a stop.

What was he doing? He raked his hands through his hair, his fingers trembled against his scalp and he quickly tucked them into his pockets to hide the emotion they exposed.

He had so much he wanted to say, but it wasn't his place so he tried hard to hold back. "Is the mare okay?" he asked instead, masking the anger and worry raging inside of him.

"Yes, she's just anxious." Her fingers went to her temple and she rubbed.

Cole wondered if she realized she was touching the place he'd kissed. He realized it. His fingers curled and he dug them deeper into his pockets.

"She didn't mean to harm me. Lucky just started barking while she was hurting and it simply got too crazy for a minute."

It *was* crazy out here. "So what's the plan?"

"The plan?"

"Yeah, are you going home or what?" He wasn't surprised when her brows dipped ominously.

"I'll be staying here, watching her. I may need to help her along from the look of things." She walked to the stall, studying the mare.

Her limp wasn't bad, but it could have been. And that was what mattered. He had a choice here. He could explode and get nowhere with her. Or…he strode toward the end of the stable.

"That's what I thought," he said. "Good thing I brought dinner."

"Dinner?"

"Yeah," he tossed over his shoulder. "Someone has to make you take care of yourself."

Her growl of frustration followed him to the end of the barn.

"I don't need you taking care of me, Cole Turner. Just because for some unknown reason I've had accidents when you were around does not mean I need you."

He halted at the doorway. "That may be so, but it's clear you need someone," he shot back.

Stubborn woman made him nuts—yeah, nuts, that was exactly what he was.

She got to him more than any woman ever had…and it wasn't a good thing.

Chapter Thirteen

Calm down. Calm down. Calm down.

Samantha nudged her arm as Susan tried to get a rein on her temper. Big, cold lips nibbled at her arm, as if to console her.

"Don't worry, girl. I'm fine. It's him who might not live through the next few minutes," she said. Understanding seemed to flow from the donkey's big brown eyes. Samantha was known for her almost human qualities. She had a wonderful sense for when someone was in need. Susan wasn't the first person for whom she'd saved the day. "Thank you for helping me, you little darling."

Lucky had followed Cole outside and now Samantha spun and pranced like a show pony on tiptoes. Her hooves tapped down the long concrete alley between the stalls like a plump ballerina.

Susan followed, glad she hadn't gotten kicked in the head and wasn't seeing two dancing donkeys.

Cole was right. She'd been stupid.

But the very idea of his being right fired her irritation all the more. She'd been totally irresponsible coming out here alone. With practically no cell-phone reception to speak of in this part of the country, she might very well have been kicked in the head or gotten a broken leg or something and been stuck out here all night. Hurt and alone.

Or dead.

She grimaced and took a step toward the outside where Cole had disappeared around the edge after telling her she needed someone. Needed someone—as if she didn't know that already! Didn't he understand she was looking? Of course he was talking about an assistant… She was going to look for one of those, too.

Movement didn't hurt as much as she feared when she marched forward. Her pride had sustained the worst damage.

It hadn't escaped her notice that God had been watching over her. It was a blessing that Sweet Pea hadn't stepped on her worse than she had.

Glancing down at her shirt, she was glad to see that it hadn't been ripped too terribly by Sweet Pea's clawing hooves. There was hay everywhere, though, and she dusted it off as she walked, her shoulder tightening up with each movement.

"What are you doing here, anyway?" she asked, disregarding the way her heart skipped at the sight of him beside his truck. She had a lot to ignore as instantly the feel of his arms around her came pushing into her thoughts. The feel of his lips against her skin—her breath caught at the memory. She'd been too stunned earlier to think about it, but now there it was. He'd had his arms around her and…and *nothing*.

She shoved the thought away. "Why are you here?" she demanded more adamantly.

He lifted a couple of boxes from the seat of his truck and grinned.

His grin caught her off guard and might very well have caused her insides to melt like warmed butter *if* she'd let it. But oh, no—she fought that sensation off with a vengeance!

"What's that?" she asked, recognizing Sam's to-go boxes even as she asked the question. Food. Food was good.

"Jake was at Sam's when I got there and he said, from the looks of the mare, he felt like you had an all-night affair—little did I know I was going to find you being hauled out of harm's way by Samantha."

His expression darkened and she knew he was fighting off saying more. Instead he held up the boxes. "Anyway, here's your supper."

She wanted to tell him so badly to take his supper and hit the road, but her stomach roared like a hungry lion.

He cocked a brow. "Don't even try telling me you aren't hungry. Not with your stomach cutting up like that." He walked past her to the mesquite bench swing next to the entrance of the barn. "Sam said you drink your tea unsweetened. Hope that's right," he said as he passed her again.

"Um…sure," she managed through clenched teeth as a new issue hit her. "So everyone knows you brought me dinner?"

"Oh, yeah. Sam insisted." He brought two paper glasses from the truck and sat down in the swing. Placing the glasses on the ground in front of him, he patted the seat beside him. "Come on. I don't bite."

So he said! Susan eased into the swing and took the box of food he offered her. Might as well eat and hopefully then he would leave. The aroma of barbecue brisket caused her stomach to let out another roar, this time so loud Lucky's ears lifted as he plopped at her feet and waited for handouts. "This smells wonderful," she admitted grudgingly.

"Yep. No matter where I go I always miss Sam's cooking." Cole opened his box, closed his eyes and inhaled. "That is Texas gold right there. *That's* what I'm talking about."

Susan almost choked watching him. His dark lashes rested against tanned skin and his lips were turned up at the corners... Gracious, she couldn't stop staring! "Yes, I know what you mean." She sighed. His eyes popped open and she dropped her gaze to her box—snapping the lid open so fast she almost threw the food off her lap. Lucky barked and wiggled, thinking he'd very nearly hit the mother lode.

Needing something to do other than think of how handsome the ornery, oh-so-bossy cowboy beside her was, Susan grabbed a roll and chomped on it. She could only hope Cole didn't notice that unlike Lucky, she wasn't thinking about barbecue.

Maybe she had been kicked in the head after all!

"Why are you so stubborn?"

His irritating question shouldn't have surprised her. It did. "If a man conducted his business as I do, there would be nothing said about him being stubborn. He would just be taking care of business. You, Mr. Turner, are just—"

"Yeah, I am." He held her gaze unapologetically. "Sexist. Is that what you were about to say? Because if you were and it is— I know you—then so be it. If me thinking you don't take good enough care of yourself puts me in that category then I'm in and proud of it."

Unexpectedly his words sent a longing so strong through her that it took her breath. She chomped into her roll and chewed as if dogs were chasing her. *Do not let your guard down. Don't do it!*

He was bossy and irritating, but he was trying to look out for her. Trying to protect her…and it felt oddly nice.

Not since her dad had she had anyone want to protect her.

A lump formed in her throat. *Whoa, stop right there. You are moving to Mule Hollow hoping to find someone who can put up with your way of life. Someone who can love you despite it…not someone who thinks your life is all wrong.*

They ate in silence for a few minutes. She wasn't sure where to go or what to say, so she just ate. Her head was full of thoughts. She placed a piece of meat in her palm and held it down for Lucky, then rubbed his head after he snapped it up. "You love your job, don't you?" she asked, because it was the easy question. The safest question. It wasn't the one asking why he didn't stick around in town or settle down. That was what she really wanted to know…why hadn't Cole Turner settled down? *Maybe because he's so ornery!* Well, that was the truth, but she knew God made partners for even the orneriest of them.

He reached for his drink; in the glow of the big light on top of the barn she watched him shake the ice around. "I'm not sure if I'd call it love."

That struck her as odd. "But you live on the road. You go from place to place—I just assumed you loved it."

"I help people. I like that. Don't get me wrong. But..."

But what? She toyed with her food then closed the lid and placed the box on the seat between them. "But?" she finally asked, intrigued when he remained silent. She watched his Adam's apple bob.

"You love your job?"

She nodded. "It's pretty evident."

"Yeah. Anyone who dedicates almost every waking hour to something and totally ignores her safety has to love something."

"So we're back to that." Disappointment shrouded her as new anger flared. "I need to check on Sweet Pea," she said, pushing out of the swing, glad her hip didn't protest too much. "Thanks for the dinner."

"That hip hurting a lot?" he asked, following her out of the swing.

"No. I've been kicked and stomped on before. It's—"

"Part of the job," he said, disgust dripping from the words as he finished her sentence for her.

"Yes. It is," she snapped, stalking into the stable, trying not to limp too noticeably. What did the man expect from her? A person couldn't be a vet and not expect to get dirty or kicked a few times…or tired. She shot him a glare when he fell into step beside her.

"Look—" he started.

"No, *you* look." She turned on him. "I don't need you strutting around here judging me. This is what I do. This is who I am. If you can't accept that, then I really don't need you hanging around. I didn't ask you to come here. And as for lunch tomorrow—forget about it. The offer is retracted. And if you're thinking about hanging around tonight, don't. This isn't my first foal and it won't be my last." Her knees were shaking as she stormed away. Her daddy had told her she'd have to sacrifice things to get what she wanted out of life and she was willing to do it. If she didn't get rid of him now, she might regret it. For the first time in her life, she was scared she might be tempted to give up more than she wanted. All this fear he had for her was stifling. *Wasn't it?*

Cole was not good for her. Not good at all.

"Go home," she insisted. "And I mean it. Get out of here."

Cole raked his hands through his hair and watched Susan disappear inside Sweet Pea's stall. He'd really overstepped his boundaries this time. What was it about Susan that had him tied up in knots with concern? Sure she'd had a couple of accidents when he'd been around, but things happen. She couldn't live in a glass cage—

What was he thinking? He walked to the stall, boots dragging as he tried to figure out what he should do.

What he needed to say. When he reached the stall he saw that Sweet Pea was down and the birth had started. Only a few minutes earlier the mare was struggling, and now in the blink of an eye the foal was coming. Susan was down beside her helping and he started inside to help her, but she shot him a glare, jerked her head in the direction of the barn exit and had him stopping in his tracks. Clearly she was serious about wanting him to leave.

So be it. He spun and strode to his truck. Susan didn't want him hanging around and she had things under control. He, on the other hand, didn't have anything under control. Nothing at all.

"Wyatt, are you coming to town or not?" Cole paced the floor of the stagecoach house. When he'd first arrived home, he'd stared at his Harley for twenty minutes before talking himself out of hitting the road back to Galveston. Instead he'd decided it was time to call his big brother—after all, it was Wyatt's fault he was in this mess.

"Sorry, brother, but I'm not making the trip. This case—"

"Don't even go there," Cole growled. "Seth already told me about the plan to get me here and then keep me here."

"I'm not denying that," Wyatt said. "I thought it would be good for you. It's time for you to come home, Cole. You used to love that place out there. Until Lori. I really was coming home to talk to you face-to-face about this, but I'm tied up with an unexpected turn in this case. I'm about to board a plane to New York right now. But listen to me, Cole. It's time to let Lori go. It's time to stay home where you're needed."

"I'm needed—"

"At home. That's where you're needed now, and where you should stay long enough to come to terms with whatever's hounding you."

"I'm not hounded." Cole leaned against the counter and stared at the hundred-year-old cabinets in front of him. His roots ran deep here in this cabin and on this land. But his heart— "I need to leave, Wyatt."

Wyatt didn't say anything for a long moment and the clock on the mantel ticked off the seconds. Every second weighed on Cole. He needed the road. He needed… what? This wasn't the same as the other times—this was different.

"How's the remodel coming along?" Wyatt said at last, breaking into Cole's troubled thoughts.

"I'm getting there."

"If you're thinking about leaving, remember you signed up for that job. Running away isn't going to help that pretty vet get into her place. It'd be real sorry of you to leave her high and dry."

"What are you, my mother?" Cole ground out.

Wyatt chuckled. "No, bro, I'm your big brother and don't you forget it. You are my responsibility and I keep tabs. So how's the good doctor?"

"She's an ill-tempered, stubborn woman who is probably ruing the day she hired me. I know I'm not too happy about signing on. Whoever that contractor was that skipped out on her, he must have gotten a tip-off that working for her wasn't going to be a walk in the park."

That got a big hoot on the other end of the line. "So y'all are getting along that well."

"Well? We barely tolerate each other, but—" Cole broke off, shifted his weight from boot to boot, and frustration clawed at him. "Wyatt, I can't stay," he blurted out at last.

"Why? Because you're attracted to someone?"

"Ha—like a moth to a flame!" He was doomed if he stuck around. It was a no-win situation.

"That's better than living half a life."

"You have no idea." Cole's temper was rising. As kids growing up, Wyatt had always been the leader. He took his position as eldest seriously and Cole knew it had taken will-power on his part not to step in and try to fix Cole's problems beforehand. He'd obviously realized that what ailed his baby brother was beyond even him. Cole hoped he kept thinking that way.

"Cole, I've stayed out of your business for six years. But I'm done. Talk to me."

"You can't fix everything."

"Maybe not but that doesn't mean I'm going to give up. You know me—when have

I ever given up on anything that I thought was important?"

"Never." It was true and Cole knew it. Cole suddenly had an uneasy feeling. "Wyatt, what have you been doing?"

"Whatever I needed to do. Do you remember I was at Seth's wedding, too?"

That was weird. "Well, duh."

"Duh is right. I was standing beside you most of the night, remember?"

"Yeah, what does that have to do with anything?"

"You were only there in body most of the night. And then Susan walked in. For the first time in a long time, I saw life in your eyes when you and the Doc locked gazes. I sure thought it was interesting."

"You would," Cole drawled, but couldn't help smiling. The Turner men came from a long line of men who enjoyed "campfire stories." Wyatt could hold his own up against the best of the best and often did in the courtroom.

Problem was, this wasn't the courtroom. This was his life and Cole wasn't exactly certain what to make of Wyatt's little fairy tale.

"You need to ask her out. The two of you

need to talk."

"No."

"Ask her out, Cole. Not to work at the clinic or to work cows. Ask her out to a nice place. It'll remind you about what it's like to sit down in a nice restaurant with a lady and enjoy a good meal."

Cole had just eaten with Susan and there wasn't anything about the experience that could be called pleasant. "If we went out to a restaurant, it would probably end in a public fireworks display, compliments of the temperamental doc. No, thank you."

"Don't leave, Cole." Wyatt's words resonated across the phone lines. All teasing was gone. "The Cole I grew up with was fearless and tenacious and had a heart that was ten times bigger than mine…. Stick around and finish what you signed up to do for Susan. You can't run when someone else needs you. You've never done it before and I know you won't do it now."

Cole looked at the floor and shook his head, hating that his brother knew him so stinkin' well.

Chapter Fourteen

The Mule Hollow Church of Faith was a quaint, whitewashed church built back when the older folks of town had been kids. It had always given Cole a sense of homecoming when he entered the front doors. He could still remember as a boy being hustled into the fourth pew on the left by his mother as she lined her family up to worship the Lord. His cowlick would have been slicked down at least four times before he'd picked up a hymnal. By the time the preacher got up to give the message Wyatt would have already told a couple of jokes under his breath to make Cole and Seth giggle…and their dad would have already shot them "the look" that said sit up and get right.

Memories here were good ones.

When he'd left for college, the town had been the color of dried-out cardboard, wind-blown and struggling. The church had held about a hundred and fifty people in boom times, but wasn't even half-full now. Most of the kids his age weren't planning on coming home after college. Not unless they were like Seth, who'd never wanted to be anything but the man who kept their heritage alive for the next generation. People like Seth, Clint Matlock, Norma Sue, Esther Mae and Adela and their husbands had been the ones who kept the dying town alive for people like him to come home to…eventually.

"Can you believe the crowd?" Applegate said, meeting Seth in the doorway and handing him a bulletin. "It's done grown since the last time you were here," he boomed, obviously without his hearing aid, since half the church would have been able to hear him if it hadn't been for Adela on the piano banging out "Give Me That Old Time Religion."

"Yes, sir, it has," Cole said, running a hand over the cowlick that seemed determined to relive old memories.

Seth stepped up beside him and grinned. "Mom had fits with that cowlick of yours."

"Yeah, I've tamed it pretty good but walking in here always brings back memories."

"You boys better hurry or your pew is gonna get taken."

"We're waitin' on Melody," Seth said. "She had nursery duty during Sunday school—"

"I'm here," Melody called, coming up the steps in a rush. Her cheeks were a pretty shade of pink and her dark hair seemed to accent them.

Cole watched Seth kiss her on the cheek and give her a hug as she placed a hand on his brother's heart and whispered something in his ear.

"No kidding?" Seth said, looking amazed by what she'd said.

"It's the truth. She just told me," Melody assured him.

"Told you what?" Applegate bellowed, not in the least bit embarrassed for having butted in.

"You'll see. It's not for me to tell."

"But ya told Seth." Applegate's thin face fell in a cascade around the frown.

"That's because he's my husband and we're one and the same."

Cole thought Seth was going to burst he

looked so happy as he took Melody's arm. "That's one of the beauties of marriage. We better take that seat."

He looked around the room for Susan, but didn't find her as he followed them down the aisle to an empty pew—not pew four but five—his brother was shaking things up, it seemed.

He shook hands with Stanley, who was sitting in pew number six with Pollyanna and Nate Talbert, and he shook Nate's, too. He was turning back around when he saw Susan enter the back door. She wore a red dress and when she smiled at Applegate, he wished it had been sent to him—a wish he didn't want to have. The notion was like a kick in the gut, so real that for a minute he lost his breath. He spun toward the front and stared at the choir. Made up of mostly cowboys and the match-making posse he found himself staring straight at Esther Mae. Her red hair was topped with a white hat with pink daisies that matched the hot-pink dress she wore. But it was her sparkling green eyes and her possum grin that had his attention. Beside her, Norma Sue, in her blue-striped dress, was smiling so big her plump cheeks almost touched her eyes. He frowned, realizing the cowboys standing behind them had their eyes glued on Susan as she found a seat.

Cole's eyes narrowed on the cowboy at the end.

"You thinkin' of taking him outside?" Seth asked through the side of his mouth. "Or you just giving Norma Sue and Esther Mae something to talk about?"

"Huh." Cole stiffened and saw the two singing ladies grinning at him. Okay so he was losing it—what had gotten into him?

"Yeah." Seth chuckled. "I'd tone that down a notch if I were you."

Cole scrambled to grab a songbook. Was he jealous? The question rolled around in his head the whole time. To be jealous you had to have feelings for someone. Did he?

Pastor Allen took the podium. God seemed to smile through him as his gaze swept the gathering. Seth hadn't been to the church since he'd taken over, but he could feel good vibes from the older man. "We have an exciting announcement this morning. Ashby and Dan went to the hospital last night and delivered a healthy baby girl!"

A wave of clapping ensued. "God has been good and is building the church and the town population. This is exciting. As you know, Lacy and Clint Matlock want a baby and have been trying for over a year now to do their part to build the congregation. Lacy, why don't you tell them?"

Everyone had already turned toward the couple. Lacy was beaming as she hopped to her feet in the middle aisle. "God is just so awesome. We're finally having a baby, everyone!" she exclaimed and threw her arms around Clint and kissed him.

At the news, Esther Mae squealed like a schoolgirl and Norma Sue did, too. They scrambled over their husbands, practically knocking them down to reach Lacy and swallow her up in hugs. Adela left her pew beside Sam and followed them. She had the most satisfied expression on her genteel face as she took Lacy's face in her hands and kissed her cheek.

Melody leaned around Seth. "This is wonderful news! She wanted to surprise the ladies here in the sanctuary because she felt like God had brought them all together and it was important to share the blessing here to give Him honor."

Minutes later, after everything had calmed down, the pastor gave a great sermon on giving God the praise and the glory even when times are rough or life isn't turning out as you expected. He used Lacy and Clint as an example, in that they'd been praying for a baby for some time, but they'd had to wait until God made the way. The pastor emphasized that the couple had walked the walk of Proverbs 3:5, "Trust in the Lord with all your heart and lean not unto your own understanding." That even when it looked like they might not have a baby, they'd worked hard to trust God in the situation. Even when it wasn't easy.

Cole swallowed hard as the words rolled around in his mind. He'd trusted the Lord and hadn't had a happy ending… Oh, he'd gone on with his life, but there was no way he'd ever understand why sweet, spirited Lori had suffered and died so young.

"Come on Cole, stay for lunch and volleyball," Norma Sue said after services, blocking the path to his truck.

"Sorry, Norma Sue, I'm not hungry and I haven't played volleyball in years," Cole hedged, angling toward his truck.

"You might as well say yes," Seth said. "Norma's not going to let you go. Don't you remember she gets every cowboy who ventures through that door out on that sandpit? Give it up, bro."

"And besides," Norma Sue snorted, "I remember you used to play a mean game of it, so pretending you don't know how won't cut it with this ole gal."

That made him grin despite the disquiet churning inside of him. "I didn't say I couldn't play. I said I haven't played in years."

"It's just like riding a bicycle."

Seth grinned, enjoying watching Cole lose the discussion.

"Besides," she added, "we have to celebrate Lacy and Clint's news and if you leave that'd be mighty rude of you."

It would be a distraction from the memories, too. "I'll stay," he drawled. "But, be warned, I'm not going down easy. I remember that you might be short, but you set well and serve fierce."

Over the top of Norma Sue's head he saw Susan out in the parking lot getting into her truck. "Hey, I'll catch y'all inside if you don't mind." He sidestepped toward the parking lot. He needed to talk to Susan. Norma Sue and Seth both glanced her direction.

"We don't mind at all. And fair's fair,"

Norma Sue said. "You go grab that gal and bring her back here."

"You do that." Seth chuckled. "And don't take no for an answer."

Cole dipped his head to them, spun on his heel and jogged the distance to Susan's truck. She'd already started the engine and he slapped the side to get her attention. "Hey, hold up," he called, rounding the fender. "Where do you think you're going?" Skidding to a halt in the white rock, he smiled at her and placed a hand on her open window.

She lifted her hand to shield her eyes against the sun that was high and bright behind him. "I have too much to do at home to stay and play."

He didn't miss the curt tone—and understood his behavior at the stable elicited it. "Nope. If I have to stay then you have to stay," he coaxed, feeling lighter just looking at her, knowing he wanted to bring a smile to her face. Norma Sue had had a great idea; a play day would be good for Susan…and him. Might even help him forget some of the heavy things on his mind.

"Ohh, no. I certainly don't."

"Okay, I get that hanging with me is the last thing you'd want to do. But c'mon, it's Sunday. You're supposed to rest on Sunday, remember?" He went to open her door but she grabbed the windowsill and held it in place. "It'll be fun and you know it. Besides, Norma Sue told me not to let you go anywhere." He tugged the door open as her eyes turned to cute, feisty slits. He smiled— couldn't help it. Man, he felt good suddenly.

Her shoulders sagged slightly. "Cole. I really don't feel like it."

"Look, if this is about last night, you were right, I stepped over into your business. I still think you put yourself at risk, but it's not my place. This is your life. Stay. It'll be good for you and I'll leave if it'll make you feel better."

She expelled a heavy sigh of frustration. "Don't be ridiculous. Your leaving isn't necessary. I'll stay." She snapped the ignition off.

He pulled the door open wide and held out his hand to her. "Let me help you, ma'am," he drawled.

"I can make it on my own," she said and slid from the seat. "And *believe* me, a few minutes into this game, you'll be needing *my* help."

* * *

Susan watched the ball descend toward Cole on the other side of the net. Taking a step, she gauged her defensive move to his. He stepped then jumped into the air—she left the ground a split second later, arms up. Just as he hit the ball, she hit it right back at him—he missed the shot and looked shocked as the ball landed at his feet like a cannonball.

"The girl can play," Cole said, grinning.

"Ya don't need ta take his head off," Applegate yelled from the sidelines as laughter and loud whistles erupted.

Susan ignored it all, intent only in keeping Cole Turner from making any points off her.

She hadn't actually wanted to hang around if he was going to be here. He'd made her so mad out at the barn the night before that she hadn't been able to sleep. But dad-gum the man sure was cute grinning back at her through the net.

As the game started up again, the voice in the back of her mind chattered like it had all night long—*he was simply concerned for her.*

It was nice to have someone concerned for her—or at least she'd *thought* it would be nice. She'd never thought about how a husband's overprotectiveness could hinder her work. Not that Cole was remotely being considered for the job—still, it had her disturbed more than a little bit.

"Susan," Esther Mae exclaimed from the left of her. "Your ball! Your ball!"

Susan jerked back to attention and spotted the ball just as it whizzed past her head. "Sorry," she grumbled.

"Where's yor head?" Stanley called.

"It ain't on her side of the net," App grunted.

Susan cut her eyes at him. "I just lost my train of thought for a minute—"

"We saw that," Esther Mae said. "Cole must be up there winking at you just like I told him to do."

"What?" Susan asked, glaring at Cole. He was grinning like a schoolboy.

"She suggested it, but I'm innocent. I told her a wink from me would only make you madder at me and then you'd really whip us for sure."

She arched a brow in agreement. "You got that right."

His smoky-blue eyes brightened and he chuckled. Delight wrapped around her heart—unexpected and aggravating. She did not want this, but it was as if God was playing an April Fool's joke on her and she was falling for it hook, line and sinker.

"Game ball!" Norma Sue bellowed, holding up the ball that would win the game for Susan's team if Cole's team didn't hit Norma's serve.

Though she was a short, robust woman wearing boots, rolled-up jeans and a headband that had her kinky gray curls rivaling the look of Richard Simmons, the woman was deadly on a volleyball court. Cole hadn't expected the game to be this big a battle.

Across the net, Susan hunkered down into position and gave him the look—the one he'd come to realize in the past hour meant she was about to try to eat his lunch.

"Cole, better watch out," Stanley called from the sidelines. "I'd be plumb embarrassed if she got two in a row past you."

"Yep, yep," Lacy yelled from over by the food. "You better dig deep, Cole Turner."

Seth chuckled behind him and Esther Mae harrumphed beside him. "You can do this, Cole. If it comes my way this time, I'll get out of your way. I don't want you knocking me over again."

Him knock *her* over—Cole cut his gaze to her in surprise and when he came back to Susan, her eyes were twinkling—that was good at least. She'd seemed to have difficulty gaining focus at the first of the game, but then she'd come out swinging and he'd been hard-pressed to defend his position at the net. She was excellent at spiking the ball and had several times nearly taken his head off when she'd leaped into the air and slammed the ball. He kept getting distracted watching her fluid grace.

Of course only now did he learn she'd put herself through vet school on a volleyball scholarship—a nice bit of info he'd somehow missed.

Norma Sue tossed the ball then slammed it, sending it skimming straight at him—he was well aware that it was a deliberate hit that would have him and Susan fighting at the net. He and Susan rose as one to block the other's shot at the same time. The next minute he felt wind by his ear as she drove the ball back past him straight into the ground.

He grinned as he landed. "Well done, Doc."

She laughed. "Not so bad yourself, cowboy."

"I think that means the loser buys the winner a soda," he said as everyone swarmed about them in a flurry of congratulations and consolations.

She hesitated. "I guess it would be kind of sorry on my part as the winner if I turned down an offer like that."

"You're right. After beating the socks off me, it would look pretty bad to tell me no. In fact, I think it should be lunch." He was thinking of the date she'd canceled—the one they were supposed to be having now.

"So are you saying *yes?*" Cole asked, thinking he'd misunderstood, since she'd agreed so easily.

"Well, it's the sportsmanlike thing to do," she said as she headed toward the group gathered around the tables.

Cole was quick on his feet. Moving as if he was dodging an angry bull, he shot out in front of her and blocked her path. "Oh, no, you don't. I just worked entirely too hard for this lunch date and I'm not looking to entertain a crowd anymore today."

She studied him with slight mistrust in her eyes. "So what exactly do you have in mind?"

Chapter Fifteen

Susan held on to Cole's waist and couldn't help but enjoy the feel of the sun on her face and the wind in her hair as they rode through the beautiful hillside. Riding with Cole on his motorcycle was the last place she'd expected to be…or wanted to be. Wasn't it?

She blinked against the wind and tightened her hold around his waist as they rounded a curve. Playing volleyball reminded her that she was moving to Mule Hollow to try to begin a new life. To try to *have* a life. Following volleyball with a motorcycle ride was a good way to start…Cole just might be right.

There had been much teasing and a flurry of excitement as Adela and Lacy threw together a sack lunch for them and hustled them on their way. It had been embarrassing.

As they headed toward his black-and-chrome Harley he'd smiled at her and made her smile when he told her that he'd enjoyed watching her have a good time, even if it was at his expense.

The man had a way about him—when he wasn't being a domineering oaf—that seriously drew her to him…dangerous thing to admit but it was true. He was so different from his brother Seth. Susan had thought at one point maybe she and Seth would have made a great couple. Seth was so settled and sure of his spot in life that they'd gotten along great from the moment she'd first begun working in this area and they'd become friends. He'd been in what she'd thought was a serious relationship and then when he'd broken that off, she was dating someone—of course that didn't work out. But when they both were single and she'd thought now was the time, he'd fallen for Melody. She'd been happy for him, but sad for herself. She'd not been able to help thinking that she might have missed out on the best man she'd ever known.

The man she could have trusted would never leave…but the first time she saw him and Melody, she knew they were meant for each other. There was a beautiful spark between them. That "thing," that unspoken connection, that everyone around a man and a woman in love can see. She couldn't help but be thrilled for them.

At their wedding when Cole had walked in, she'd thought instantly, "Now, there is a man."

He was nothing like his brother, oh, no. One look at Cole and she'd felt as though she was stepping out on a tightrope. With Seth she felt an easy feeling of comfort. Not anywhere near the tightening of her stomach, accelerated heartbeat and the we're-going-over-the-edge-of-the-cliff feeling she got when Cole was near…

That impression had solidified and done nothing but gather speed since he'd come home. Being around him was always like a roller-coaster ride. But it was all surface stuff.

So now here she was with the sun on her face and the wind in her hair as she took this step to get to know him better. She was terrified…her daddy had always told her fear was her best friend if it helped propel her forward. Susan had no idea if forward was good in this situation but forward she was determined to go.

She had to find out if this spark she felt when she was around him was what she feared it might be…

Energy filled Cole as he jogged down the old stone steps to where she stood on the large flat rock that jutted out into the water. The river swerved around the rock and rapids gurgled and swirled as the rock ledge on both sides of the area narrowed. Susan shielded her eyes and looked at him.

"I never knew this was back here," she said, amazed. "Can you imagine what a welcome respite this must have been for those stagecoach passengers a hundred and fifty years ago when those stages rumbled to a stop at the house?"

He looked about thoughtfully, taking in the beauty and the timelessness of the place. "I've thought of it often. Actually as a kid I'd come here to this spot for respite myself. It's special."

"I can see you here," she said, her eyes sharpening with interest. "I bet you dreamed of all sorts of things."

He tucked his hands in his pockets—the logical way of keeping them from reaching out to her. Which was suddenly exactly what he wanted to do, right here at his special spot. He'd never brought anyone here before. But he'd made the decision to share it with her the instant she'd agreed to have lunch with him.

He held up the plastic grocery bag Adela had handed to him before they'd left. "Are you ready to eat?"

"I can't believe they threw that together in the few moments we were telling them we were going for a ride."

"Adela and Lacy are quick-handed women, is all I can say." He led the way along the wide rock to where another ledge made a good place for them to sit. "As a kid, I pretended this was my thinking couch."

She sat down with a space between them for the sack of food. Scooting back so her feet dangled, she leaned against the wall. "It reminds me of one. All we need are a few pillows to soften it up a bit."

He nodded as he extracted two bottles of water, some turkey sandwiches and a large, half-full bag of chips from the sack.

"This looks good," he said, his mind racing for an opening.

Susan nodded. "Can I ask you something?"

"Shoot away." His interest spiked instantly by the hesitancy he heard in her voice.

"When you were sitting here, did you dream of settling down?"

There was his opening…as if God was telling him to open up like he'd wanted to do.

He laid a sandwich on the napkin Susan had just removed from the sack and placed in front of him. He steadied his thoughts. "I didn't. I dreamed of being a rodeo star and seeing the world. I brought my rope here and I practiced to the sound of the water rushing by."

"That's kind of what I'd put together about you," she said before taking a bite of her sandwich. She looked away, studying the water as it flowed past.

"But things change."

"How so?"

"First, I never figured I was needed around here. I love this place, the land, the fact that it has been in our family all these years. I love coming home to it—"

"But you hardly *come* home. I mean, at least since I've bought the clinic and been doing work around here, you haven't been home much."

He grinned. "Been keeping up with me even before you knew me. Impressive."

"Yeah, you wish." She laughed. "That *Seth* has mentioned you a time or two is the *only* reason I even knew you existed."

"There's no need to be embarrassed. I'm sure my gals, Norma Sue and Esther Mae, have mentioned me to nearly all the single gals just like yourself. They're always looking out for a suitable match for their favorite prodigal son."

She shook her head. "Hate to burst your bubble, but they never once mentioned you to me."

He let out an exaggerated sigh. "And here I thought they were on pins and needles waiting for me to come home to roost."

"Don't feel too bad. They've been busy with all the cowboys *already* living here."

"This is true. Still, I'm wounded."

"So—it wouldn't really matter. Right?"

"Actually, at the time I left it, it wouldn't have. The rodeo team at college was my ticket to see more of the world. I never meant to leave home forever. But my third year at school I met—" He had to pause as emotions slammed into him at the thought of meeting Lori.

Susan's gaze went still and she studied him with open curiosity. "Who?"

"A very special girl. Her name was Lori and she'd been on the team the year before I signed on." After all this time it was just like yesterday. "She was an excellent barrel racer and sister to one of the ropers. And, well, she'd had to drop off the team due to a rare form of cancer. The team admired her and dedicated most of their rides to her so even though I'd not met her, she was there in spirit every time we went out."

Susan placed her sandwich on her napkin and listened, unmoving. He studied her thoughtfully, her healthy glow and vitality so in contrast to Lori's sallow coloring when they'd met… "She came to the arena one day. She'd lived longer than the doctors expected her to and had beaten the odds, as some would say. She gave all the glory to God for every second she was alive. And she believed God had kept her alive for a reason—she was convinced of that and had been trying hard to figure out what it was that day when she walked into the arena." Cole took a shaky breath, remembering that moment as if it was thirty minutes ago.

"She changed my life in ways I never thought possible. She was frail—so frail I thought she might need to sit down to catch her breath as she walked up the wheelchair ramp to the bleachers."

"What happened? Did she make it?"

"Yes. She made it into the stands and sat on the bottom bleacher and watched the practice. I roped my calf, but when I went off my horse to tie his hooves she let out a whoop and I slid in the dirt and went down. I was laid out flat on my back in the dirt and heard her soft chuckle. For the first time in my life, I didn't care that I'd missed." He smiled. "All I could think about was going over and meeting the girl I'd heard so much about." He glanced at Susan and widened his smile…thinking about how hearing that rich laugh coming from such a fragile woman had affected him.

"She must have been a great gal?"

He shook himself out of his nostalgia. "That's all I could think, too. I mean when someone makes an impression like she had on so many, it gets a person's attention."

"So what did you do?"

"I picked myself up, dusted myself off, walked over and…and, I gave her my heart." He swallowed hard and caught the surprise in Susan's face. "Yeah, hard to believe, isn't it?"

"You fell in lov—" Her voice caught, which caught him off guard. "You fell in love?" she asked, her voice hushed.

"Like a rock." He leaned elbows on knees and hung his head. "When I looked up through those arena bars into her eyes—so shadowed and hollow, but…extraordinarily full of life—I knew I would never be the same." He wasn't exactly sure why he felt so compelled to open up to Susan about Lori but it felt good to talk to someone. Why her? Maybe it was so that she would stop and take less risk with herself. Not take her life or the quality of that life for granted.

"Was she recovering? In remission?"

"No." He gave a slow head shake as he held Susan's startled gaze. Sure she was probably unable to believe he had the capacity for something like that—he hadn't known it himself. Feeling compassion for someone in that situation was one thing, falling in love in a heartbeat—some would say was crazy. And they had said it plenty. Pushing forward, he continued—details were hard. "We had three months. People called me crazy. Who would pursue someone who was dying? If I could, I wouldn't wish it on anyone. But I wouldn't change it for me. Lori was the best thing that ever happened to me."

Susan's pain-filled eyes bored into him but she didn't say anything.

"She taught me what was important. Look, I've never told anyone all of this. I don't exactly know why I brought you here to tell you this, but I did. Life is precious. You should enjoy it and take care of yourself. There is more to life than your career. Don't take it all for granted."

Susan's heart hammered with Cole's words. The man had fallen in love with a terminally ill woman—it was heartbreaking. "What did you do?"

He rubbed his knee, as he seemed to go back in time thinking. "I'd hurt my knee and was struggling competitively in my rodeo events. My dream was dying and it had been killing me. But after meeting Lori, it wasn't important anymore. I started seeing things in black-and-white in terms of importance. Which makes it even more difficult to handle what happened after she died…

"I shut down and for a while nothing was important to me, nothing at all. Thinking about those weeks now, I'm ashamed because I feel like I let her down. She'd wanted me to let her go easily. She'd been prepared to die. But even knowing this, there was no way—" His words died abruptly and he turned his head away from her.

Susan's heart broke for him. She wanted to comfort him, touch his shoulder, something, but she couldn't move.

"I couldn't understand how someone so wonderful had to go through so much," he said, his words harder, his eyes flat when he turned back to her. "I still don't. It's a part of life I don't get." He shook his head in distaste. "I didn't mean to get into that, that isn't why I started telling you this. I was just trying to let you know that you need to take care of yourself. Do more of this type of thing. Play volleyball, laugh. Hire an assistant who will be with you when you go out on call. You shouldn't be so stubborn about it."

So that was what all of this was about— he slipped that assistant in there so smoothly. What exactly had she hoped it was about?

More.

The man had just given her a look inside his heart and even said he didn't do that with many people. No one in town, other than

Seth maybe, knew this side of him. She would have heard something about it…she remembered Norma Sue saying she thought something had happened to him, but she didn't know what. Now, Susan knew and she'd felt touched, even honored, that he would confide something so personal to her. He'd just described giving his heart to Lori in an unbelievable instant. He'd still stepped over that line and given his heart to her, knowing that he would suffer such a void after her death. But obviously he hadn't confided in her because he felt connected to her…

Oh, no, hardly. She blinked and stared away from him. Had she really thought his telling her meant more than it did? And why, oh, why did she care? She knew he was merely trying to use the experience to get her to slow down and hire an assistant.

"You want to know why I'm so stubborn?" she asked, more disappointed than angry at his continual soapbox stand on her life. "I understand the void you feel. Not exactly in the same way but, still, losing people you love is hard. Even with God's comfort. My mother died giving birth to me. She was forty-five. They'd wanted a child so badly, but had given up years earlier and so when my mom found out she'd conceived me she was ecstatic. She was cautioned to give me up because of some complications, but she refused. She basically gave her life to bring me into this world." The very idea of it had truly overwhelmed her growing up. Her mother hadn't had to die for her. But she'd loved her. "I always think of Jesus when I think of my mother's sacrifice. Jesus died on the cross for us because He loved us so much, and my mother died in labor because she loved me so much. Even though she'd never seen me. It's overwhelming sometimes when I think about it."

Cole took her hand. The contact was so unexpected it took her breath.

"I'm so sorry for your loss," he said, his smoky-blue eyes darkening like gray skies before a rain.

Susan felt his sincerity and as she looked into his eyes she felt comforted. "Thank you." His hand tightened about hers and his thumb soothingly caressed her skin. "My daddy and I were everything to each other. He was fifteen years older than my mom, though, and he felt like I needed to be able to stand on my own two feet in case something

happened to him. He died just after I gradu-
ated high school and was getting ready to
enter college. Though he'd prepared me, I
still had lessons to learn." Had she ever.
Thinking about how hard those years were
reminded her not to feel bad about her stub-
bornness. She'd been alone and grieving
when she'd entered college. She'd also felt all
of her father's expectations while feeling lost
at the same time. "I'm stubborn and determined and driven for a reason, Cole. Yes, I'm
moving to town to try to have a life. But I
can't change who I am." And that was what
he would have her do—she pulled her hand
from his. "I am the child my father raised.
Knowing your story helps me see why that
bothers you. But I will make my father proud
in my short lifetime." She stood up, too
troubled to stay seated. "I think we should go
back now."

She'd confided too much and knew it had
simply been the result of a long two days…a
long two weeks. That was it.

He would be through with the clinic by the
end of the next week if he hurried it up, and
then he'd move on. He'd be gone. Back to the
altruistic life he'd chosen after losing the love
of his life.

All she had to do was not think about that. Not think about how she would love to be the one to take away the pain she'd glimpsed in his eyes as he'd talked of Lori.

Chapter Sixteen

"So how's it goin?" Sam asked on Tuesday morning when Cole walked into the diner with Seth. From their seat at the front window, Applegate and Stanley tuned in. They called out a "howdy" and leaned a bit closer to make sure their hearing aids picked up all bits of conversation.

"Don't ask," Seth said. "Cole might bite your heads off."

Cole shot him a grumpy glare as he took a stool. He'd avoided the diner on Monday because he knew he'd get the fifth degree from the old fellas. He'd already gotten it from Norma Sue, Esther Mae and Adela. The three ladies had visited the clinic first thing Monday morning. They hadn't even tried to hide their real reason for dropping by and had immediately begun drilling him about Sunday afternoon.

He'd told them little. What was there to tell? That he'd opened up to Susan and had completely come across the wrong way. She'd empathized with him over Lori but hadn't gotten why he'd told her…he wasn't sure he completely understood why he'd told her.

The last thing he'd expected was for her to reveal what she had. He'd had no clue what she'd been through and he seriously doubted that anyone in town knew that she'd lost everyone so close to her…early in her life. No wonder she was so independent.

"I'm almost done with the clinic, if that's what you mean," Cole offered.

Applegate spat a sunflower seed into the spittoon. "I heard Susan was out most of the night last night," he boomed. "She was back and forth between here, thar and yonder with one emergency after the other. You seen her?"

"Nope. She hasn't come by."

"That ain't good," Stanley yelled across the room.

Sam set cups in front of Cole and Seth. "Nope, sure ain't."

"She's busy. It's her job," Cole snapped, watching as Sam filled his with coffee. "Thanks," he grunted. He took a cautious swallow. Black and caustic, the coffee burned all the way down his throat and settled in his stomach like acid on acid. He took another swallow.

"Shor she's busy but…" Sam drawled. "It still ain't good that she's burning both ends of the candle. The little gal is dancin' with disaster if ya ask me."

Cole couldn't agree more. He wasn't the only one in town who thought she put herself in dangerous situations. Or was stubborn. Or needed someone to watch over her. She might be a certified veterinarian, but she was a woman alone at all hours of the night and no matter how she explained herself to him he could not and did not think it was safe for her.

Chauvinistic—maybe by some people's terms—but to him it was just plain and simple fact that any woman he cared about was going to have to understand that he'd have her safekeeping in mind at all times. Who, at night, would know if she didn't return home after being called out on emergency? Who would know until she didn't show up for work that she had run into trouble? Had a wreck? He yanked his thoughts away from her and her business. Or at least he tried. The woman was starting to obsess him. She seemed close to Betty but still she lived all the way in Ranger.

"Earth to Cole," Sam said, topping off Cole's coffee. "Did she say when her new equipment is gonna arrive? From what I gather, she did real good in the sale of her other place. Got all new stuff comin' for the new clinic."

"I don't know about all that, but whatever it is it's supposed to arrive Saturday. I'm working to get everything ready for it."

Applegate stood up and ambled over to the counter. He was moving slow—limping, too.

"Is something wrong, App?" Cole asked, noticing the way the older man was moving.

Stanley spit several sunflower seeds into the spittoon. "We been helping Norma Sue bottle-feed some ornery baby calves." Stanley chuckled. "One of 'um got the better of ole App yesterday."

App grunted. "I'm still sore. The calf decided it was a goat and tried to mow me down."

"That's the truth," Stanley agreed. "If Norma Sue hadn't grabbed it when she did, ole App might'a got the boot right out of town."

"Now thar's an idea," Sam said, rubbing down the counter.

Cole chuckled listening to them. They always gave each other a hard time. But since they'd all been friends for sixty years or more, it didn't look as if they were gonna split up or anything.

"So when you movin' back here, Cole?" App asked, ambushing Cole with the sudden change of subject.

"I've told him I need him," Seth said.

Cole shot him a hard look. "I'm enjoying what I do."

"Humph," Sam snorted. "From what I hear you ain't even got a home ta call yor own out thar. Livin' in a hotel room ain't no life fer a man. Especially when he's got responsibilities back home and good reason fer being there. Yor brother is a newlywed—you should thank about him and also yorself."

"That's right. Just like I jest did by beatin' the socks off this old sourpuss," Stanley said, jumping several of App's checkers. "Remember roots are good. Especially fer raising kids."

"That's what I'm telling him," Seth said.

Cole drank his coffee in silence and let them carry on with their ambush.

A few minutes later after avoiding answering their questions and making his escape, Cole and Seth left the diner. Cole couldn't help thinking that roots were good. Having people around who cared about you and knew you so well they could say anything— might drive some folks crazy but knowing those folks cared about you was a nice feeling. That was what Mule Hollow was made of.

"Some things never change," he said as he climbed into Seth's truck.

"Nope. It's a good feeling, isn't it?" Seth's eyes were serious beneath his Stetson.

Cole gave a short half laugh. "You're trying real hard to make me reconnect, aren't you, brother?"

"You know I am. I want you here, Cole. Plain and simple. It's more than just about me needing you at the ranch. It's where you belong. You always said you were coming home to raise a family. So come home. Settle down. Find a good woman and have that family. Lori would have wanted that for you and you know it."

Cole didn't want to get into this and yet… it was unavoidable.

"And what about Susan?" Seth prodded. "If I'm right, there's something there, isn't there?"

"Drive, Seth."

Seth slapped the steering wheel. "I was right. I knew it," he said. Cranking up the truck, he backed out. "What are you scared of?"

"Nothing."

"That's a lie and you know it. Come on, Cole. Talk to me."

"I have obligations—"

"You and I both know you don't have anything going that you can't get out of. And, besides, even if you did, it's easy enough to plan to come home as soon as those are up."

It was true. He'd freed himself up before coming here but there was plenty of work that still needed doing. "You know as well as I do that I can walk away from life as I know it at any minute. But that doesn't mean I want to."

Seth shot him an irritated look. "Why, because coming home would mean you'd be tied to responsibilities that aren't so easy to get out of? You'll never find peace unless you make a stand, Cole. You have to stop running."

It would mean, also, that he'd be in town—around Susan…as of Sunday he wasn't sure if that was a good thing or a bad thing. "Out on the road I'm able to be happy most of the time…. I'm managing. I'm helping people." And any disgruntled feelings that would besiege him from time to time could easily be pushed aside and ignored while he worked at solving other people's problems. "It's a good way of life for me. Here. Honestly, Seth, I don't know how it would be. I don't know if I can handle it."

And Susan. Well, Susan complicated the situation tenfold.

Seth pulled the truck to the side of the road. "Cole, you can handle anything. With God's help, you can conquer this fear or sadness or whatever it is. You are not alone. I know without you telling me that you blame God for taking Lori. And I know you felt powerless watching it happen. But, Cole, you have to know you deserve to move forward and have a life, too. One built around roots and family and not driven by anger and sadness and emptiness. You're my baby brother and

I saw you when we lost Mom and Dad. When you hurt you bottle it up. You hold it in—you smile and joke but it's there. Truth is truth, Cole. And the truth is, it's time to stop."

It was seven in the evening when Susan turned into her new driveway. Cole called to say he needed her help with something, but he hadn't told her what it was. She'd been out nearly all night and was dragging, but her energy level surged upward dramatically on seeing him standing in the doorway.

She'd thought about him almost constantly ever since Sunday. But she'd stayed away. She wanted to be the woman who took away the pain she'd glimpsed in his eyes. It was a dangerous thing to be thinking.

He wore his tool belt today—a reminder that, yes, he worked for her. His lean jaw was scraggly with stubble as if he'd been working as many hours as she had. His wavy brown hair curled from beneath the ball cap and his eyes seemed to light up as she approached. She couldn't help thinking that the smartest thing she could do was get back in her truck and race in the opposite direction.

But she was no chicken. Or at least she'd never been before. "Hi," she said and smiled, feeling self-conscious about all she'd revealed to him about her past. She was still amazed that she'd done that.

"I'm glad you could make it out, finally. I hear you've been busy the past four days."

She couldn't tell if he realized she'd been avoiding him or if he really thought it had all been about being busy...she went with busy. "Very. So what's up?" she asked, keeping her focus.

He moved aside and let her pass into the building. The caustic scent of stain and varnish hit her. It wasn't strong enough to cause her eyes to tear up or to run them out of the building but it was there making itself known.

"You look— I, well, I had an idea that I wanted to run by you."

She almost smiled at the way he'd changed course on telling her she looked tired. Because it was more than obvious that was exactly what was buzzing around in his mind. The fact that he'd decided against saying it was good, so she pretended not to notice as she followed him to the reception desk.

The place looked fantastic. The cedar walls looked beautiful and the cabinetry he'd done in pine, opting to clear-coat it so the wood would show and match the light weave of blond running through the red of the cedar. He'd done her counters in the same wood and they looked very rustic.

"I still have to finish out the bathrooms and some cabinets in the dispensary and surgery. The front area is done, except for adding a clear coat to the front of the reception desk and the counter. I waited to do that because I had this idea about putting a few brands on them first. What do you think?"

Susan's interest peaked. "That sounds interesting. Like take a bunch of different people's brands and burn them into the wood?"

"Exactly!" He beamed at her. "I figured you'd get the idea pretty quick. What do you think?"

"I *love* the idea. I really do." She met his smile with one of her own and time just sort of sat there between them. *Focus, girl, focus.*

"Good," he said. "I had a feeling you would. Follow me," he drawled, crooking his finger and then heading toward the doors leading into the back area. "I took the liberty to round up a few irons and thought since it's your building you should have the honor of doing the first brand."

Oh, boy—wasn't that thoughtful? A warm

sense of pleasure filled Susan and she hushed the small voice yelling "focus" in her head. He had several branding irons heating in a gas warmer and she pulled a few out and recognized the brands. "I really love this idea." It seemed to be the only phrase she could string together at the moment.

"I'm assuming you've handled irons before?"

"Actually, no."

"Really?"

"Yeah, don't do branding. Some vets do, some don't."

"Not a problem. I'll show you how it's done."

"I really— That sounds great," she said, catching herself before she repeated herself again.

He grinned. "Then we had better get busy. Are you driving back to Ranger tonight?"

She heard the "you don't need to" tagged onto the end even though he didn't say the words. "No. I'm staying here, at the house."

"That'll help us get this done, although this shouldn't take more than a couple of hours. Hopefully you won't have any emergency calls and you can get some rest."

The man had tried, but hadn't made it five minutes. But instead of it irritating her as much as before, she felt that same sense of pleasure flowing through her. He seemed genuinely to care about her overworking— if she relaxed a bit, she'd admit that it was a nice feeling. *Wasn't it?*

"What brand do you want to start with?" he asked.

"Is the Triple T in there?" she asked, knowing that was the Turner Ranch's brand.

"Right here." He pulled it from the batch and handed it to her.

"Then that's it, in honor of you thinking of this and also for getting me out of a bind."

"I really love that idea," he said, his eyes twinkling as he mimicked the way she'd said the words.

She liked the teasing side of him. "Where is Cole and what have you done with him?" she asked.

He reached for a brand, his smile fading. "It's all me. I can have a lot of fun when I'm not stepping over into someone else's business." The side of his lip hitched upward again. "But when a lady isn't watching out for herself it's kinda hard for me to keep my mouth shut."

She thought of Lori and wondered if he

was, too. "I think…that's an irritating, but commendable quality—"

His eyebrows shot upward in surprise. "Susan? Is that you?"

She gave a short laugh at his startled words. "That doesn't *mean* I like being bossed around," she warned him, giving him a look, "but I know you mean well."

"I do, Susan."

She heard the sincerity in his words and she believed him…. Her heart caught realizing how much she wanted to believe his actions for her were motivated by more than just concern.

She took a breath and looked at the brand in her hand. It was time to change the direction of the conversation or take the chance of exposing her emotions.

"Are you okay?" he asked.

"Y-yes. I think this brand has grown cold." She struggled to sound normal. It was a hard thing to do when she felt as if she were losing control of her heart.

Chapter Seventeen

Cole stared at Susan and felt off-kilter. He'd come up with this idea about the brands the day before, after he and Seth had had their little talk. He'd been in such a foul mood that the last thing he wanted to do was spend time with Susan. Nope, he'd planned to avoid her at all cost, until he finished the job and hit the road. Which would be next week—unless he could get done early.

But this idea was too good to pass up. When it hit him he'd known he was going to have to put off clear-coating everything and call Susan to come out to get her opinion and her help.

Looking at her now, he was almost overcome with the desire to pull her into his arms. He stepped back. He was leaving. Nothing good could come from testing the waters between them. He wasn't looking for that. He was interested in keeping her safe. And in getting her into her building.

They'd had to put the Triple T brand back into the heater to fire it up again.

"So how do you do this?" Susan asked again as they waited, sounding as if she was searching for something to fill the awkward silence between them.

Cole went with it, needing the distraction. "When you press the iron to the wood, you have to keep it steady. Give it even pressure and it'll do the work. It's easy. You ready?"

She nodded.

"Then let's do this." He pulled the brand from the heater and handed it to her. Their fingers brushed, drawing their gazes together. He let go instantly. Heading back inside, he held the door for her to pass. "I'm glad you came," he said, unable to not tell her the truth.

She paused, her eyes serious. "Me, too. I should have come out more. I—I didn't mean to abandon you during this project but I— Well…" She swallowed hard and he could tell she didn't know how to move forward.

Welcome to the party.

"Anyway, I'm glad I came." She hurried

through the door and once inside she studied the front of the four-foot wall of the reception desk as if her life depended on getting this right.

Susan was just as mixed-up about what was going on between them as he was. At least that was what he thought. She was probably even more intent than him to keep this business—like she'd said from day one. She'd been right about that. But denying his feelings was getting harder and harder to do. And that was not something he'd anticipated.

Finally, Susan positioned the Triple T's brand almost perfectly in the center and pressed. The muscles of her arms tightened as she leaned into it.

"You're doing good," Cole said, enjoying watching her. Susan liked to get things right. It was obvious in the way she applied herself to anything she did. He liked that, despite worrying about her. He'd come to realize there was much about Susan that he liked, which was exactly where all of this other emotion was coming from.

"Thanks." She studied the brand, now burned black into the blond wood in a nice contrast. "It's just a tad off on one side, don't you think?" Leaning her head slightly to the right she contemplated her work.

"You aren't going to lose sleep over that, are you?" His teasing got him a glare…but unlike other times, this glare instantly faded to a smile.

"I'm not *that* much of a perfectionist."

He grinned. "That's a relief," he said, teasing yet totally truthful. "Come on. What do you say we get this show on the road?"

"I say let's do it!"

They got new irons, and Susan walked back into the front area. She stared at the desk for a long moment and wondered if she was going to line it up perfectly with his brand. He hoped she would do what he'd envisioned and start branding the wood in random order…some slanted, some sideways, some straight.

"Here goes nothing," she mumbled, then pressed the brand at an angle.

Yes! He laughed then took his brand and pressed it beside hers.

"Now, that looks good. Once again, great idea, Cole Turner."

"Glad to be of service, Doc. It's working out better than I thought it would."

It was true, he realized. It had been a long few days and he'd missed her…

The idea flowed through him as if trying to settle in where it wasn't welcomed.

He *had* missed her. Very much…

And no matter how much he was trying to deny it—or put off that he was merely feeling things out of concern or in friendship—he couldn't. Question was, what did it mean? What did he want it to mean?

Susan was trying hard to act normal and not let Cole see the conflicting emotions she was fighting. She'd been doing that a lot lately. Focusing on the branding helped, but when he suddenly grew quiet she raised her gaze to his, just as his brows crinkled and his eyes dimmed.

She couldn't move as he took a step toward her. The ringing of the phone broke the silence, but not the tension of the moment. When the phone rang in the evening it was usually the dispatch office with an emergency call. Reaching for it, she couldn't help thinking she had an emergency going on already…one she was not at all prepared to deal with.

Turning her back to Cole, she listened as the dispatcher relayed the message. She could feel Cole's eyes staring at her the entire time.

"What's happened?" he asked the moment she hung up the phone.

"Mrs. A. is at the emergency room in Ranger with a broken hip. She's demanding to see me." Her heart was pounding as she headed for the door.

"Hold on, let me cut off the furnace," Cole said, racing out the door into the back area again.

She didn't slow down. She was already behind the wheel of her truck when he came jogging outside.

"Wait up," he demanded, slamming the clinic door behind him.

"Cole," she protested through the open window, snapping her seat belt into place. "I don't have time! I have to go. She won't let them operate until I get there." She knew he was thinking of coming with her. She didn't need the distraction, and she started to back out.

"Don't you dare back up," he warned, jogging to the truck even as it moved away from him.

"Cole—" She pressed the brake as he yanked open the passenger door and slid into the seat next to her.

"Now drive," he growled.

She glared at him. She didn't have time to argue with him. And she didn't appreciate him just—

"Would you stop looking at me like that and just drive? I'm not going to mess anything up, if that's what you're worried about."

Easy for him to say, she thought as she hit the gas, shooting the truck back like a bullet. Stomping the brake hard, she pulled the gear into Drive, pointed the front end toward Ranger and floored it.

Beside her Cole flew forward then was yanked backward against the seat.

"You might want to put that seat belt on," she snapped.

"Ya don't say," he drawled, but reached for his seat belt.

She glanced his way and he cranked a brow up and casually stretched an arm across the back of the seat. He looked entirely too settled. Entirely too comfortable—

"Maybe you need to look at the road," he advised, ever so calmly, nodding toward the road ahead.

She planted her eyes forward immediately and had to swerve to keep from running off the shoulder!

She half expected him to say something smart, but instead he just asked, "Did they give you any details about Mrs. A.?"

"No. It was my evening answering service and they didn't have much info. Just that she needs surgery but she insists on talking to me."

"I hope she'll be okay. Any clue what she wants you there for?"

"Not sure, unless it has to do with Catherine Elizabeth. I don't know why else she'd request me."

"Do you want me to drive?"

"Cole, stop!" She scowled at him. "Don't start that. I'm telling you right this minute that I'll pull this truck over and kick you straight out of here if you go mothering me."

"Mothering you?" He held up his hands.

"Yes," she warned, feeling more like herself.

"Okay, okay. I'm behaving. But the offer is there."

Susan grunted and kept her mind on the road. She was worried about Mrs. Abernathy. She didn't need to have the aggravation of Cole Turner riding shotgun beside her, butting into her business—making her think about how he'd looked only moments ago when she'd thought he wanted to kiss her. *No!*

She just plain and simple didn't need him. He was all wrong for her…had been since he drove into town, and nothing had changed.

Except it feels nice to have him, doesn't it?

She bit her lip as the notion tangled her up inside. This was not the time for this. Not the time at all. And yet he was here…but he wouldn't stay. She had to protect herself from that. She had to. *Didn't she?*

He reached over and turned on the radio. The sun had gone down and the night air whirled about them as it whipped through the open windows. The unromantic scent of stain and clear coat had seeped into their clothing and now the scent swirled about them— maybe all those fumes were the reason for her weird thoughts.

She suddenly was wishing there was more time for them. More time for him to be around…and more time for her to get him to see things her way. If the man could understand her viewpoint they might be able to act on this crazy attraction…or at the very least become friends. Because despite his irritating stand against her way of working, she still couldn't get over that fact that the man's heart was big enough to fall in love with a dying woman. And then big enough to devote his life so far to helping others… But no matter how much they didn't get along, there was just too much about the man for her to admire. Even if he was stubborn and totally ignored what she wanted.

It suddenly hit her—had he been this way with Lori? How had she felt about him falling in love with her? Had it given her something to regret leaving behind? Had it made her dying harder?

Chapter Eighteen

"Oh, you brought your man with you!" Mrs. Abernathy said the minute Susan and Cole walked into her room.

Susan didn't take the time to point out that he wasn't her man—he just wouldn't listen to her. She was too concerned for Mrs. A. to think about Cole. She looked so frail in the big hospital bed. Especially with the IV in her arm and the monitors beeping all around her. She also looked like she was feeling no pain. They must have given her something to make her comfortable. The nurse had told them before she showed them in that they were ready to take her to surgery the minute she spoke to Susan. The nurse and the orderly followed them into the room and began getting ready to roll.

"Mrs. A., you poor thing. What can I do?" Susan asked as Cole moved to her bedside and took her hand in his.

"We're here to do whatever you need us to do," he said, smiling sweetly when Mrs. A. looked up at him with slightly glazed eyes. Tears formed as she nodded to him.

"My Catherine Elizabeth is out there alone. I need you to find her. And, Susan, I need you to fix her up for me and then keep her while I'm recovering from this dad-blamed weak hip. I tried to tell them when they picked me up that my baby was lost in the woods somewhere. But there were only two of them and they said they had to get me in the ambulance. No one would go search for her."

Distress filled the old woman's eyes and Susan's heart broke. Gently Susan took her hand with the IV hookup and gave it a gentle squeeze. "You don't worry about anything. We'll go find Catherine Elizabeth."

"Yes, we will. You can count on that."

Susan felt reassured by Cole's words. She knew the old dog's problems and worried that it might already be too late to help her. "What happened to Catherine and where should we look?"

"I was at the Stony Creek Cemetery where my Herman is buried. Catherine Elizabeth was with me. We were putting flowers on Herman's grave. I looked up and saw Catherine Elizabeth running across the country road—can you imagine my baby running? She was chasing a rabbit and looking like she was a big puppy. I started to go after her but fell and that's when I broke my hip. A car was passing by and the man helped *me,* but he wouldn't leave me and go find my Catherine Elizabeth. No one would. She's out there alone and you know she's sick."

There were tears in her eyes and her blood pressure and heartbeat had increased. The nurse stepped in. "I'm sorry, but we need to get her to surgery. We've waited as long as we can. The doctor is waiting."

Susan nodded and met Cole's stormy blue eyes. "We're on our way," he said, looking back at Mrs. A. "I promise you I'll find Catherine Elizabeth."

Susan's heart kicked up. Cole Turner was not a man to give his word and back down. She suddenly wondered how many people over the past six years since Lori's death he'd made promises to. Promises to rebuild their homes, their businesses. Their dreams.

Mrs. Abernathy had leaned forward in her

agitation, but now looking at him she relaxed. Part of that was due to the meds the nurse had slipped into the IV drip, but still, Susan could tell she had total confidence that Cole was going to do as he said.

"Thank you, Cole," she said, her words slurring. "I'll pray for her and for you to find her. Susan, will you watch over her?"

"I will watch over her until you are able to move back home and reunite with her."

"Good. Good."

The nurse nodded to the orderly and they slipped her onto the gurney.

"We'll see you when you come out," Susan said, letting go of Mrs. A.'s hand at the door.

"Don't you worry about anything," Cole called.

"Oh, I'm not now. God sent you and He's taking care of everything."

"Cole, wait up. What is wrong?"

Susan was fast on his heels but he didn't slow down until he reached her truck. "I'll drive," he said, stopping at the driver's side and holding out his hand.

"No. You're too upset."

"I'm not upset. I have a dog to find and no time for this. Now, give me the keys."

Susan studied him hard, as if trying to look inside his head, then she dropped the keys into his hand. "They're all yours. Now let's find Catherine Elizabeth."

Cole didn't talk as he drove.

"What's the matter, Cole?" Susan asked after they'd left the town behind and were speeding toward the country graveyard.

"How bad is this for Catherine Elizabeth?"

When Susan didn't answer he glanced her way. "Susan?"

"She isn't used to being outside. She could just be scared and hiding. But she could also be in trouble. I'm not sure if Mrs. A. would do well if something happened to Catherine Elizabeth. She loves that sweet dog. They are family."

Cole gripped the wheel. He wanted to believe God would take care of the old dog. Especially since it was the most loved thing in Mrs. A.'s life. But he wasn't getting his hopes up for divine intervention. He would, however, do everything within his power to bring Catherine Elizabeth home to Mrs. A. There was no way he was going to face her with anything but good news. Being in the hospital had reminded him all the more of how it felt to lose your loved one…. Mrs. A.

already knew that feeling, because she'd lost her husband. He couldn't let her go through that again.

He didn't ever want to go through it again himself.

"Cole." Susan laid her hand on his back three hours into their search. "Are you okay?"

He shrugged off her hand and moved away from her. "I'm looking for a dog that could very likely be dead."

"She could still be alive."

He shook his head in disgust. "Don't patronize me, Susan. I'm not one of your little ole lady clients you need to cheer up. We both know the odds are against her. You said it yourself earlier. If she was able to come to us she'd have already been here. She knows and loves you. The fact that we haven't even heard a whimper is not good, and you know it."

"That's true—I did say that earlier. And…" She rubbed the back of her neck and scanned the area as if believing Catherine Elizabeth was suddenly going to appear and prove him wrong. "And I was thinking the same thing as you only a very few moments ago. But, Cole, I don't think this is all about a dog. Is it?"

He frowned. "We're wasting time."

Susan stepped up close. He went totally still when she suddenly placed her hands on his face. "I believe God is going to come through here tonight," she said with full conviction that it would be so.

Cole stared into her beautiful eyes. If only he could believe that. "God lets people down every day." He took the best of the best—how then did she think he'd care for a dog? He'd taken Lori despite all the prayers. Despite all the trust.

"Do you believe that God is going to come through here tonight?" she asked.

He looked away.

"Look at me, Cole Turner," she said, forcing his face back so she was staring into his eyes. They were a mere breath apart as she leaned in and stared hard into his dead-feeling eyes.

"God said to have confidence in Him," she said sternly. "Remember 1 John 5:14 says, 'This is the confidence we have in approaching God, that if we ask anything according to His will, He hears us.'"

Cole broke away from her. "Don't talk to me about confidence. I learned the hard way that God takes what He wants and it doesn't matter what kind of confidence I have in Him."

"Yes, it does."

"No, it doesn't. I prayed for Lori and I had confidence that He was going to work a miracle and heal her. I trusted Him then, so don't start with all of this. He gets to do as He sees best. But He can't expect me to put my heart on a platter and believe He's going to answer my most heartfelt pleas. I can't play that game anymore."

He couldn't. "I rely on the abilities He's given me to accomplish answering prayers. He might not choose to answer them, but if I'm in the picture I'm going to do everything in my power to do it."

"And you've given up on saving Catherine Elizabeth."

"Yeah, I have. It's late. She's old, sick and more than likely she's out here curled up somewhere dead." Susan wiped a tear from her eyes and knelt in front of him. "What are you doing?"

"I'm going to pray, Cole. You're right. God has the right to do what He wants. But He is going to do what is best…for everyone. Not just for you and your selfish wants. But for everyone. He knows the future. He knows what is coming in the lives of all those around. You don't know what He saved Lori from in the future. You don't know how many people she touched as they watched her live—from what I've learned from you—was an extraordinarily close walk with Him during the days of her illness. How many lives did she touch? How many lives did her unerring faith change for the better? She felt like every day she was alive was a gift. You told me that. I had that with my dad. He knew every day we had together was precious and a beautiful gift. And he prepared me for life after his death. He prepared me for every way possible and I've been hard-nosed and determined to be the woman he prepared me to be. But you know what, Cole? I forgot something until this very moment. He prepared me most importantly for his passing by giving me a strong faith. He knew when he died that I was going to be okay. I'd forgotten that he told me to be strong and stand up for what I wanted but that without God on my side none of my accomplishments mattered. I believe God sent you Lori as a gift. He knew He was taking her home for reasons we will never know or understand. But He gave you those precious, beautiful three months together. I think Lori recognized them for what they were and she tried to prepare you."

"So what are you praying for?" His question was a bare whisper.

"I'm praying that God is going to show you a miracle tonight." She held up her hand to him. "Come pray with me. Please."

"Susan," he said. He couldn't believe she was doing this. "This is useless."

"Please, Cole. Come down here. Please."

This was the last thing he'd expected from Susan. He couldn't move. What she'd said about Lori weighed heavily on him. Lori had touched every life she came in touch with. She had been a gift. He'd felt privileged for every second he'd had with her. She'd felt the same way. But this was about believing in God answering his prayers. And He hadn't answered the one that meant the most to him.

Susan took his hand and continued to look up at him. "God tells us to ask and believe, Cole. To ask and believe and then trust that He is going to do what is best. I'm going to pray Catherine Elizabeth is okay and that we are going to find her. And I believe with all my heart that if it is His will, that sweet dog is going to come walking out of the shadows, and her return will show you that He worked all things out for good where Lori's life was concerned."

Cole couldn't move. He stood still with Susan's hand grasping his so tightly it hurt. She smiled gently up at him then bowed her head and prayed.

Cole stared at the top of Susan's bowed head. His heart was thundering in his chest and he closed his eyes. She believed. She really believed. He prayed for her sake that God would answer her prayer. But he didn't hold any high hopes that it was really going to happen.

He opened his eyes when she finished to find her smiling at him. He pulled her up and hugged her. She melted against him and wrapped her arms around him. He felt her comfort and strength flowing through him. He kissed the top of her head. "Thank you for that. But—"

"No buts, Cole. No doubts. God is going to provide. I feel it."

He glanced around and saw nothing in the darkness. There was no sound other than the crickets and the tree frogs. There was no sign of Catherine Elizabeth and no sounds to say she was near. "Come on, Susan. It's time to go back to the hospital and check on Mrs. A. She's going to need us."

Susan rested her head against his shoulder and her heart pounded against his. *Please, God, show this man that You had a plan for his life. That You let a beautiful soul into his life not to leave him sad and discouraged but to give him hope and to make him into the man You wanted him to become.*

She looked into his eyes then glanced around. There was nothing. She wanted to be disappointed but she'd prayed for God's will to be done. She didn't understand what that plan was but she had to trust that He was working it out for Cole's benefit. And God was not her puppet on a string.

"I'm ready. God's will be done."

"You tried," Cole said as he kept his arm around her shoulders and walked her out of the woods. "What is Mrs. Abernathy going to do?"

Susan sighed as he tugged her closer to comfort her. It felt good to be comforted by him, but... "I don't want to believe that Catherine Elizabeth is dead. But if she is, Mrs. A. will be fine. She was strong, so strong when her Herman died. She is a woman of faith and I don't believe you've realized that about her."

"I'm glad to know that," he said.

They stepped over a log and headed the last few steps to the edge of the woods. Susan tried not to cry, but her heart was heavy for Cole. She wasn't sure why she was so compelled to prove this to him. But again, God's will be done.

She blinked and wiped tears from her eyes as they stepped out of the woods. Cole stopped and went still. She looked up, and there wagging her old gray-tipped tail was a grinning Catherine Elizabeth.

Chapter Nineteen

Cole pressed the last brand into the counter and waited as the hot iron burned its way into the wood. From her pallet in the corner Catherine Elizabeth watched.

"So what do you think, ole girl?" he asked. Pulling the brand away, he moved to stand beside the dog. He scratched her ears as he studied the front of the pine reception counter. "It has a certain charm about it, don't you think?"

Catherine Elizabeth barked and turned her head so she could nuzzle his hand with her cold nose. He still couldn't believe she'd been sitting there right in front of them the night before.

Susan had been convinced that God had answered her prayer to prove to him that He cared for Cole. That He'd had a plan for Lori's life and for his. Susan was convinced of all kinds of things the old dog's miraculous survival was supposed to prove to Cole. Truth was, Cole didn't know what to think. When Mrs. A. had awakened from her successful surgery he'd been overjoyed to tell her that her old companion was alive and well.

"That must have been some rabbit hunt you went on last night," he said, bending down to look into her chocolate-colored eyes. He'd volunteered to keep her at the house with him and then bring her along to work.

"All that worry and you were taking a nap," he said, giving her one last rubdown before heading out back to turn off the branding heater.

He couldn't stop thinking about Susan dropping to her knees like she'd done. He'd fallen to his knees like that and begged God to save Lori.

He'd bargained and pleaded with God to spare her. To heal her. His prayers had gone unanswered. He was glad for Mrs. A. that Susan's had been answered.

Cole pushed the memories out of his head and went to finish installing the fixtures in the bathrooms. It was the last of the work here…once he finished the cabinet doors in there and put the top coat on them and the reception desk he'd be done.

And he could hit the road.

He needed to do that as soon as possible. He knew if he stayed around much longer, he'd have to admit that he'd fallen in love with Susan.

And he couldn't admit that.

Couldn't let his heart open up that much. Couldn't chance setting himself up for the heartache of losing the one he loved ever again. He'd been afraid Mrs. A. was going to have to face that last night over Catherine Elizabeth. She'd already lost her beloved Herman and no matter what Susan said about her being a woman of faith, he'd seen the terror in her eyes when she'd feared for her dog. He'd known that fear as he'd walked out of that hospital. He'd remembered it as if it was yesterday and, faith or no faith, Cole couldn't willingly open himself up to that ever again.

It smelled as though Cole had just clear-coated the reception area. Susan walked into the clinic later that day and smiled as she looked at the room. She loved the cool mix of rustic functionality—the branded desk was one of the highlights.

"Cole. Catherine Elizabeth," she called as she pushed open the door to the back. The place still smelled of clear coat even with fresh air billowing in from the open bay doors.

"Cole," she called again, looking up to see if he was in the ceiling working like he'd been that one night.

"Hey, Doc," he called, peeking around the door of what would be the women's restroom. Catherine Elizabeth came ambling out to greet her. Susan dropped to her knees and gave her a hug. She looked good, as plump as a plum, but good. Cole had been sweet to keep her with him so that she wouldn't be so lonesome while Mrs. A. was recovering. It was amazing how much peace it had given Mrs. A. knowing she was going to be with Cole. To her, even just the outward appearance of him was reassuring. He was a walking, talking hero. Mrs. A. told her this morning that God had sent him to take care of her Catherine Elizabeth. She'd also said that he needed healing and time.

Susan had been startled when the older

woman had taken her hand and told her that. Her perception had amazed Susan…or perhaps Susan was wearing her feelings on her sleeve now, and if she wasn't careful everyone might be able to see that she'd fallen in love with Cole Turner. Obstinate, hardheaded man that he was… It was crazy. The last thing that should have happened. But obviously love was not logical.

"I just finished hanging the last door in here. Come have a look. See what you think."

She stood but her feet seemed rooted to the cement floor as she looked at him. His hair was tousled and his clean-shaven jaw made her want to place her hand against it.

Move, she told her feet and was happy when they obeyed. *Act natural,* she told herself. Hard to do when she wanted to run over and throw her arms around the man.

Crazy. That was precisely what she was. She needed to prescribe "reality" medication for herself. Only problem was she was pretty certain they didn't make anything for humans or animals that would cure what she had.

"Wow," she said, staring at the finished room. "This is so cool."

"Are you sure you like it? Because if you

don't, I can rip the tin off the walls and install Sheetrock in a day."

She couldn't stop smiling. The walls halfway down were lined with corrugated tin. The bottom half of the room was cedar with a chair rail dividing it from the tin on top. She'd liked the creativeness of the room before, but with the cabinet doors installed, the finished product was fantastic. "Are you insane? Clients are going to love everything about the clinic. I don't want you to change anything."

"Then we're done here."

He studied her with serious eyes that caused Susan's heart to stumble. He was so close and yet she felt closed off from him suddenly— as if he'd pulled a barrier between them.

"How was Mrs. A.?" he asked.

"She's great. The doctor says with her strong constitution and determination she should make a full recovery. I told him it would take more than a broken hip to get her spirits down. I also assured her that for as long as she needed me to, I'd take care of Catherine Elizabeth."

"Good." He tucked his fingers in his pockets and nodded.

"She loved that you were watching over

her this morning," she said, feeling an urgency to break past the barrier but not sure how. "She told me— Well, she told me you were sent from God to watch over her sweet dog." She'd said that several times.

Cole's expression tensed. "I'm glad to help out, but you were the one who had the faith last night."

Susan wondered, especially looking at him, if anything she'd done had gotten through to him. She was afraid it hadn't. Afraid actually that she may have done more damage than good with her actions. She was still amazed at how God had worked everything out in His own way…she was well aware that He might have chosen not to answer her prayer in the way that He did.

"The, ah, the equipment should be here before noon," Cole said, leading the way toward the front. Taking them to different territory both physically and conversationally.

She pulled her thoughts back and followed him. "Sure. Then all it will take is a little setup and some organization and I'll be up and running."

"Sounds like a plan."

He was being too pleasant, she thought as he held the door open for her. "Thank you."

"You're welcome. App and Stanley came out early this morning and helped finish up. They put outlet covers on and cleaned windows."

"You mean they didn't play checkers this morning?" She couldn't believe it.

"Nope, said they wanted to do something for you."

She blinked at the sudden welling of tears. "They are so sweet. Even with those scowls they wear half the time."

"Marshmallows," he said, and his expression seemed less distant. Less removed.

"You noticed, too?" she asked as her heart quickened when he laughed.

"The two grumps and Sam grumble and gripe like crows bickering over cornstalks, but they've got each other's backs when it comes down to it."

Susan ran her hand over the counter and traced the Triple T brand—she'd branded it into the counter several times and liked the way it looked. Liked that it stood for the Turner men—for Cole.

Beside it was an *OT* with the *T* turned sideways. "This one is your ranch's original brand, isn't it?" she asked. She knew it was, but needed something to talk about. Something to keep the wall from going back up between them.

He stepped beside her, his arm brushing hers as he placed his hand on the counter beside hers. "Yes. It stands for Oakley Turner, my great-great-great-great-granddad."

Susan's nerves jangled as an electric current of connection flowed from his shoulder to hers. "Do you play poker as well as he evidently did?"

"Nope. Not a gambler. Or a horse trader like he was. The man could sell a man a horse and throw in a saddle to sweeten the deal. The buyer wouldn't even realize he was buying a saddle he already owned until he'd already paid the money and Oakley was hotfootin' it down the road."

Susan laughed. She'd heard many stories about the Turner man with the questionable morals who'd founded the ranch from a poker win. Seth had no respect for the man, yet loved the land. She traced the brand and her hand touched Cole's as she traced the *O*. "How," she began, sounding like a frog, "how do you feel about your granddad?"

He shrugged and let his finger fall into the trail behind hers. She swallowed and her stomach tilted.

"I'm with Seth on the subject. Oakley was pretty sorry when it came to life skills. He could lie and swindle with the best of them and probably gambled away his family's food money on more than one occasion. No one can figure out how a woman like my great-great-great-great-grandma Jane could have fallen in love with a man like that."

Her hand had stopped tracing the brand and Cole's hadn't. He drew his finger right to the tip of hers then stopped with their fingers touching. It was excruciating for Susan. "A person can't control who they fall in love with," she said softly. "Maybe Jane had no control. She fell for the local bad boy whether she wanted to or not." Just like she had—not that Cole was a bad boy.

The truth settled over her once more like a noose around her heart. She was in love with Cole Turner and it couldn't be denied. He'd loved and lost and she seriously doubted that with the way he'd described his journey to love anything else would ever stand up to it in comparison.

She pulled her hand back and put some distance between them. Her knees were weak as she forced her legs to propel her across the room to a safer distance. Safer—but not safe.

He hated her way of life and didn't understand her actions—and yet illogically that didn't seem to matter. Love and logic didn't play from the same deck.

He would be leaving…and he would take her heart with him and never know it. Of that she would make certain.

She blinked hard as she pretended to study the trim work surrounding the window. "So, you're done?"

"Yes."

How could a simple flat answer be so devastating? "I'll write you the last check and you'll be free," she managed and was startled by the steadiness of her voice. She shouldn't have been. She was her daddy's girl, pulling from the reserves of strength he'd empowered her with so well. "When will you leave town? I'm sure you're needed and missed. Wherever it is you're going."

She was moving to Mule Hollow to get a life and that life was about to ride off into the sunset. She pushed the thought from her mind.

"I'll be leaving in the morning," he said quietly. "I returned a couple of calls this morning to set up a few appraisals in a tiny town near the Louisiana boarder. It still has lots of displaced families living out of temporary trailers."

"I see." It was all she could manage as she closed her eyes, praying for God's strength. Her own wasn't going to be enough to get her through watching Cole leave. It was ridiculous.

Cole would leave and she *would* get on with her life.

It wasn't as if she'd really known him long enough to fall *madly* in love with him. Not the kind of love where she couldn't live without him…that kind of love— Well, that kind of love took time.

Drawing her shoulders back, she told herself she was really feeling infatuation. That was it exactly. "Well, then," she said, "I'll write you that check, that way you won't have to wait around any longer. I'll take Catherine Elizabeth and you'll be free. More people than me need you now— I mean—" she coughed with embarrassment "—other people need you. Now that you've finished here."

Chapter Twenty

"So he's leaving," Norma Sue said, sliding into the booth beside Adela and looking across the table at Susan.

Susan nodded. She'd decided to stop by Sam's and have lunch sitting down in a booth. It had pleased Sam no end that she'd come. But then Esther Mae and Adela had joined her. And now Norma Sue. At this point, Susan wasn't sure what she'd been thinking when she'd come. She should be at her clinic waiting for the afternoon delivery of her office equipment but after Cole walked out, check in hand, goodbyes said, she hadn't wanted to be alone. If she stayed alone she would have fallen to pieces.

And Susan Worth did not fall to pieces.

Beside her Esther Mae's expression fell. "That's what Susan just said." She scanned the group. "What are we going to do? We can't just let him ride that motorcycle off into the sunset."

"I agree," Adela said, clasping her fine-boned hands together. "I think we need something to buy us some time."

"I agree," Norma Sue said, thumping her fingers on the table.

Susan looked from one to the other, her mind whirling. "Y'all, he's leaving. There isn't anything any of us can do. He's a grown man who has other places he'd rather be."

Esther Mae harrumphed. "Crazy man, what is he thinking?"

"I just don't know," Norma Sue grumbled. "We need to figure a way to keep him here for a little longer—at least until he comes to his senses."

"But what do we do?" Esther Mae asked. "Could you tinker with his motorcycle, Norma Sue?"

"What!" Susan exclaimed. "Certainly not."

"Hold on to your bloomers, Susan. *If* I could tinker with his motorcycle I might be tempted to do just that. But I don't know a thing about them contraptions. And why in the world wouldn't you want me to keep that man here?"

"Yeah," Esther Mae quipped. "Look at you, honey. You're all flustered and agitated."

"That's right, dear," Adela said. Her eyes twinkled mischievously—very un-Adela-like. "You are *very* agitated and I believe *very* much in love."

She couldn't deny the truth, so Susan clamped her mouth shut. This was all very strange.

"Come on, admit that my Adela is right," Sam said, walking up with a coffeepot in one hand and mugs and cups clutched in formation in his other hand. He placed the cup in front of Adela. "Here you go, girls," he said then leaned closer. "So what's the plan?"

"No plan," Susan said. "Really, y'all. A woman has to have her pride. I refuse to have Cole Turner stick around because someone tricked him into doing it."

"Oh, you do have a point," Esther Mae gushed. "But, then again, what if he doesn't know how you feel? What if you let him go without telling him that you love him?"

"I never said I loved him—"

"*Oh,* you said it all right. Just not out

loud," Norma Sue drawled. "Now what are you going to do about it?"

"Yeah," Esther Mae said. "You're someone who works hard for what she wants. This wonderful career of yours proves it. So don't sit there and say you're just going to let the love of your life sneak on out of town because you don't want to rock the boat."

Susan started to remind them that she hadn't even said she loved him and certainly hadn't called him the love of her life—but what was the use? They had her number.

So what are you going to do?

She stood up. "I love y'all dearly, ladies and Sam. But I don't have a clue what to do. I really don't." She started for the door.

"Well, don't just run off. Let's come up with a plan," Norma Sue said.

"No, I have a delivery that needs to be met. And I need to think. But," she added, managing a smile, "thank you all for caring."

Norma Sue watched Susan leave and then she looked about the table. "We can't just sit here and let this happen."

"I'm tellin' y'all he loves Susan," Sam said. "I kin feel it. But if it ain't love yet, it's on the fast track ta bein' that way. I thank they jest need more time. If he hauls off and runs away because of whatever it is that happened to him after college then we might not ever get him back here again."

Norma Sue hunched her shoulders, and stared at the jukebox that sat across the room.

"But, Sam, Norma doesn't know anything about a motorcycle. She can't fiddle with it," Esther Mae said with a long sigh. "So how else are we supposed to keep him around?"

Sam frowned. "That thar is the problem. Maybe you gals can jest go over thar and remove a few parts."

"Yeah, you mean steal them," Norma Sue huffed. "I can just see Sheriff Brady or Deputy Zane coming to haul me into jail."

"Okay, back up and time out," Adela said gently. "We can't break the law. We have to figure something else out."

"Yor right, sweetheart," Sam said. "I wouldn't want them ta have ta arrest you— now Esther Mae and Norma he kin have."

"Not funny," Adela said. Reaching across Norma Sue, she patted his arm. "No one is doing anything to put Brady or Zane into a compromising position. We might not be able to fix this situation. If Susan isn't going to speak up then God will have to step in."

"That's right," Norma Sue said, lifting her cup. "Let's just pray something happens between now and in the morning that changes Cole's mind."

Esther Mae gasped. "I can't just sit here and twiddle my thumbs. There has to be something we can do."

"Patience, Esther Mae," Adela said, patting her friend's hand. "We have to learn to trust God just as much as everyone trusts Him."

Esther Mae frowned. "I just can't sit here. Sure, the Bible says for us to have patience and wait on the Lord. But it also says in the book of James, 'You have faith, I have deeds. Show me your faith without deeds, and I will show you my faith by what I do.' Well," she harrumphed, "I think it's time for a deed. *Or two!*"

"So you're leaving," Seth said, clearly not happy.

Cole had saddled a horse and ridden out to where he was checking calves. It felt good to be on a horse. His thoughts were troubled as he'd ridden but even so he'd enjoyed being out riding across the land he loved.

"I told you I was leaving the other day," he said, shifting in the saddle and glancing out toward the ravine where he, Cole and Wyatt had spent many a day exploring. "You'll have to hire someone else." He met his brother Seth's penetrating gaze.

Seth's jaw tightened and Cole knew he was trying not to let his anger overtake his words. Seth was like that, calm in a storm. Steady as rock.

"You miss this." He nodded, letting his gaze flicker about the land before tagging him again. "You can't run for the rest of your life, Cole. I feel like I'm a broken record, but how else am I going to get through to you? All the good works in all the world won't bring Lori back to you. Won't change the past."

"I'm not in denial. God gave me the ability to help people and that's what I'm doing."

"That's all noble of you and you've changed lots of lives doing what you do but I need you here and at the other ranch. I need you to help me. You need to put some structure in your life here on the ranch. And what about Susan?"

"What about her?"

"You don't have any feelings for her?"

Cole swallowed; he wanted to deny the question but he couldn't. He couldn't tell

Seth a lie. "I care for her. But she needs more than a man who, as you put it, is quote 'living in denial' unquote. She needs more than I can give."

"More than you can give or more than you're willing to give? There's a big difference, little brother."

Cole didn't like the way that sounded.

"Look, Cole, I had issues of my own to deal with when I met Melody so don't think I'm judging you about this. I just know that I've been blessed because I resolved those issues and took hold of the love God was offering me. I just want you to have the happiness I know He has in store for you, too. And my gut tells me Susan is the one to make you happy. Don't leave. At least not yet."

"Sorry, Seth. I'm leaving after church tomorrow. After I say goodbye to everyone."

Early Sunday morning, Cole walked out of the stagecoach house and stared at his motorcycle. For six years it had represented escape to him. When things started caving in around him, he'd tied up his loose ends quickly and hit the road.

But he'd hardly slept all night as his thoughts

and his heart fought. He wasn't so sure if hitting the road was what he needed now.

Maybe Seth was right. Maybe if he didn't make a stand at some point, he'd never come to peace with the things he didn't want to face. Was it all about denial? Was the entire past six years of helping others simply denial on his part?

The thought pained him.

He'd believed he was helping others out of a good heart when it may have simply been a coward's way of not facing issues—point-blank and real… He'd not faced the pain and resentment he felt eating him up inside over Lori. God should have spared her like He'd spared Catherine Elizabeth…and all those whom Cole had witnessed survive disaster and illness. God should have spared Lori.

He set his saddlebag on the porch and sank down on the steps. He knew Seth was trying to make him step up into his responsibility… and this ranch was his responsibility as much as it was Seth's. But could he stay? Did he want to stay?

It was eight o'clock. He'd planned to be on the road by six so he'd get an early start—or was it to avoid saying goodbye to anyone? He'd told Seth he was going to church, but he'd decided it would be better not to. He'd already said goodbye to Susan the day before at the clinic.

And he'd driven away from her with rocks in his stomach.

Susan. He was leaving her behind. His heart ached thinking about that.

He hadn't told any of that to Seth when he'd ridden out to give him the news that he was leaving.

It would have only made Seth more determined to keep him here. Cole grabbed his bag. It was time to go.

Time to stop thinking and ride.

Susan hadn't slept a wink. She'd paced back and forth all night and the fact was, she couldn't let Cole go. She'd not had the power to keep her mom or her dad with her—but she had the power to at least try to keep Cole in her life. No, she *couldn't* let him go.

Not without telling him that she loved him.

Not without at least trying to get him to stay.

The ladies were right. She'd fought for everything she'd ever achieved. Her daddy had taught her to set a goal and go after it. That meant keeping the love of her life in her life, too!

Storming off the porch, Susan had her truck door open and one foot on the floorboard when Catherine Elizabeth lumbered down the steps.

"Stay, girl. I can't take you with me," Susan called and hopped inside. A pitiful howl filled the air. "Not now," she groaned. She'd waited so late that she was afraid Cole had already ridden out of town. She didn't expect him to hang around for church. He'd realize that if he went everyone would be on his case to get him to stay. So she figured he'd probably rode off toward the sunrise. But there might be a chance that he hadn't.

She didn't have time to waste. But Catherine Elizabeth looked so sad, and lonely… Jumping out, Susan jogged over to the driver's side and opened the door. "Come on, girl. Let's go get 'my man,' as Mrs. A. calls him." And as she wanted him to be.

Catherine Elizabeth ambled over and waited as Susan bent to lift her. It was like trying to lift a cow all by herself. "Okay, I can do this," she gasped, adjusting her hold and giving it another try. Nothing happened.

Susan had to get the dog into the truck. Time was of the essence. She was a vet. She lifted animals onto exam tables all the time. She should be able to lift Catherine Elizabeth, too. Wrapping one arm beneath the overweight dog and the other around her back legs, Susan took a deep breath and *heaved...* "Don't want to hurt your feelings," she grunted as she managed to lift her, "but we're putting you on a diet while Mrs. A. is recouping."

"A smart woman once told me to lift with my knees. Maybe it'll work for you."

The slow drawl behind her had Susan almost dropping poor Catherine Elizabeth on her well-rounded bottom. Thankfully Cole stepped from behind Susan and rescued the sweet dog before injury happened.

"Where did you come from?" Susan's heart was thundering in her chest as she looked at him. All tall and broad-shouldered, he looked so rock-solid—in a much better way than Catherine Elizabeth—as he hugged the old dog. "Wait a minute." She glanced around. She hadn't heard a truck or motorcycle drive up and, examining her surroundings, she saw neither. "How did you get here?"

"Seems I ran out of gas," Cole said, gently placing the plump pooch on the ground and giving her a gentle pat before he straightened.

"Where?"

"About five miles from your turnoff."

"But…" Susan's brows dipped—*surely, the ladies did not do this*. A vivid image of the ladies on a covert mission flashed to the front of her mind. "How?"

He studied her with light eyes. "I was too intent on leaving town that I forgot to fill up."

"Thank goodness." Norma Sue and Esther Mae hadn't snuck out to his house and drained his gas tank.

He grinned. "Really. And why exactly are you so happy that I forgot to fill up with gas?"

"No, I meant—" She stumbled to a halt, about to deny that she hadn't meant that when in fact she'd meant it very much. It didn't matter that he had just confirmed he'd been in so much of a hurry to leave town—to leave her—that he'd forgotten to put gas in his tank. It didn't matter. The only thing that mattered was that he was here.

"I meant thank-goodness-you-didn't-get-out-of-town-before-I-could-tell-you-that-I-love-you," she blurted out at the speed of light. "I realized I couldn't let you leave town without telling you. I was on my way to try to stop you when you walked up. I know you don't like my lifestyle. I know you loved Lori. And I know you love what you do. It's impossible and crazy for me to even think—" She halted, as a big grin spread across Cole's face.

"Thank goodness." His eyes seemed to caress her face as he smiled at her.

"What?"

He took a step closer and placed his hands on her shoulders. "Thank goodness you love me," he said. "Because I love you, too, and I would have hated walking that entire five miles just to have you tell me it was for nothing."

"Are you sure?"

Cole laughed and tugged her into his arms. "Yes, I'm sure I love you. I've never been more sure of anything in all of my life. I was leaving and made it as far as the crossroads and I couldn't do it. I knew that this time I didn't want to leave. I was running just like Seth said. I was angry at God for not answering my prayers and too stubborn to see what a beautiful gift He'd given me in knowing Lori and loving her. You helped me see that. But I realized when I got to the crossroads that God was giving me another gift…you. I certainly don't deserve a second chance at happiness, especially since dummy me was trying to run away from you. I prayed all the way here that you would tell me you loved me, too."

"Oh, Cole," Susan whispered. "You prayed for me."

Cole took her face in his hands, so tenderly she wanted to cry—and she did as a tear slipped down her cheek. He kissed it away, his lips warm and gentle brushed across her cheek, and caused her breath to catch in her chest.

"I prayed all the way here, believing that God had a plan when He'd brought us together. *Believing* just as you'd showed me when you prayed for Catherine Elizabeth. I knew I didn't deserve it and I was willing to accept it if you told me you didn't care for me. But I believed with all my heart that you would love me, too."

"Oh, Cole. I love you so much."

"Even if I'm hardheaded when it comes to you taking care of yourself?"

Susan cherished the feel of his arms wrapped about her. It was a feeling she knew she would never grow tired of. "I decided I love having someone to watch over me.

Someone who loves me enough to want what is best for me—"

"Then in that case I'm your man. But I'm also going to want to support you in what you do. I'm proud of what you do, Susan. Don't ever think I'm not. I just want you safe and I want to help you in any way I can if you'll have me," he murmured, his lips only a breath from hers.

Susan smiled against his lips and wrapped her hands around his neck. "I'll take you for the rest of our lives," she said, and then as his lips claimed hers she sighed with happiness. In Cole's sweet embrace, with his heart beating next to hers, Susan knew God had answered her prayers and given her the blessing of a lifetime. He'd given her her very own forever cowboy. And He was giving her a future with a man who would challenge her, as she would him. One she knew would never be boring…and as she kissed him back with a love deep and true, Susan knew she wouldn't have wanted it any other way.

Epilogue

"So when's the wedding date?" Wyatt asked, his piercing dark eyes locked on to Cole. His big brother had *finally* arrived in town a week after Susan had agreed to marry Cole.

Today was the grand opening of the Mule Hollow Veterinary Clinic and the entire town was here. It was like a small-time festival with all the door prizes and refreshments and fun going on. He'd been slapped on the back so much he thought he might need to be the first in line for the beautiful veterinarian's tender loving care…not a bad idea.

"We're looking at the dates and we're pretty sure next month we're having a wedding. You're going to make it, I hope."

"Wouldn't miss it for the world. You're happy, aren't you, little brother?"

Cole smiled. He couldn't help it. "I'm happier than I've ever been. Thanks for insisting I come home when you did. God really seems to have had everything worked out with the way Susan and I met that first night. And then when the contractor up and quit like he did— Why are you grinning like that?" Cole asked, recognizing the mischievous glint in Wyatt's eyes. Growing up, he'd seen that look often.

"Tank told me he had a great time on his fishing trip—"

"Whoa, wait a minute! *Tank.* Is that the same Tank you used to play poker with?"

Wyatt hiked a jet-black brow. "Way back before I saw the light—in my wayward days, I made a bundle off that man. Seems only right that I give him a trip of a lifetime to make everything up to him."

Cole couldn't believe what he was hearing… then again, yes, he could. This was Wyatt, after all. "It was you all along! I should have known."

"I told you I'd do whatever it took to get you home," he said, clapping him on the shoulder. "When I saw you and Susan at Seth's wedding, my mind started working. I figured you two were made for each other…and I couldn't pass up the opportunity to bring you together."

Cole laughed. He met Susan's gaze across the room. They'd come a long way and were looking forward to the life before them. He'd thanked God every day for her. "How could I be mad when I have Susan standing over there looking at me with all that love?" And it was true. "Now, if you'll excuse me, I believe I'm going to go hug my beautiful fiancée—but watch out, big brother. What's best for two Turner men is better for all three—so you're next in line."

"Hold on there, Cole. Wait just a minute!"

Cole chuckled and left his brother sputtering behind him. God was going to have to step in and be the matchmaker for Wyatt because Cole had other things on his mind…Susan was going to be his priority. And besides, Cole knew it was going to take one very special woman to put up with Wyatt, and only God could be the matchmaker where that one was concerned.

Boy, would it be fun to sit back and watch.

* * * * *

Dear Reader,

Hello—I'm so glad you decided to spend some time with me and the gang in Mule Hollow! I always try to make it a great place for you to kick up your heels and escape for a few hours.

Her Forever Cowboy is the first of three books about the Turner men. I introduced them in my July 2009 book, *Lone Star Cinderella*, about Seth Turner. I love the background story in that book and felt compelled to continue the story line of Cole, Wyatt and Chance, the cowboys whose roots go six generations deep in the Mule Hollow ranch they own. We've named the three books MEN OF MULE HOLLOW, and I hope you'll be on the lookout for them during the year.

In *Her Forever Cowboy*, Cole and Susan are both hurting and struggling to heal—both are ready to move forward. As always, I love showing that God's timing is always the best timing. I pray that, whatever you may be going through, you'll trust God to take care of you and to comfort you. He loves you and has a wonderful plan for you!

Until next time, live, laugh, love and seek God with all your heart!

Debra Clopton

QUESTIONS FOR DISCUSSION

1. I hope you enjoyed this book. Did you enjoy the background story of the Turner men? Why or why not?

2. Susan was one determined woman. Why did she push herself so hard?

3. Cole traded in his horse for a Harley. He was running from his past, but helping others as he did. Why? What was it that made him do this?

4. Cole blamed God for not answering his prayers and healing Lori. His pain was exposed as the book went along. Have you ever blamed God for not working the miracle you desperately needed?

5. Susan told Cole that we don't know God's plan, or why He lets some things happen and intervenes at other times. We have to trust that He is making the right call. What do you think?

6. Wyatt and Seth wanted Cole home. Did they do the right thing—even if it was

forcing him to come to terms with his past—by being firm with him?

7. Susan prayed for Catherine Elizabeth, believing that God was going to answer her prayers. She quoted John 5:14, "This is the confidence we have in approaching God, that if we ask anything according to His will, He hears us." Cole didn't believe this. But does God hearing us mean He will answer our prayers the way we want them? What does this verse say?

8. Susan's mother died giving birth to her. How did she relate this to Jesus giving His life for us?

9. What motivated Susan to go after Cole in the end of the book?

10. Why was Susan so determined to make her father proud? Shouldn't we be this determined to make our heavenly Father proud?

11. Many readers have been waiting for Lacy (my original character in my Mule Hollow books) to get pregnant. They'd been praying for a baby, but again, it had

to happen in God's timing. It says in Proverbs 3:5, "Trust in the Lord with all your heart and lean not unto your own understanding." Lacy and Clint had to do this as they prayed for a baby. How does this verse help you when times are tough?

12. I hope the themes of this book have helped you in some way. God is there for us in the best of times and the worst of times. We are to pray, believe and trust. Please discuss how He has been there for you when you needed Him to be.

13. Susan realized after her father died that she needed family. She needed more than work. I hope you seek out your family, and if you don't have family I hope you seek out a church family and get involved. God tells us that we need fellowship. It is good for our souls. Getting involved is the key here—why is that?

14. I've been blessed by being involved with my church family. Please share how being involved with your church family has helped you.

*Scandal surrounds Rebecca Gunderson
after she shares a storm cellar during a
deadly tornado with Pete Benjamin.
No one believes the time she spent
with him was totally innocent.
Can Pete protect her reputation?*

Read on for a sneak peek of
*HEARTLAND WEDDING by Renee Ryan,
Book 2 in the* AFTER THE STORM:
THE FOUNDING YEARS *series,
available February 2010
from Love Inspired Historical.*

"Marry me," Pete demanded, realizing his
mistake as the words left his mouth. He
hadn't asked her. He'd told her.

He tried to rectify his insensitive act but
Rebecca was already speaking over him.
"Why are you willing to spend the rest of your
life married to a woman you hardly know?"

"Because it's the right thing to do," he said.

Angling her head, she caught her bottom
lip between her teeth and then did something
utterly remarkable. She smoothed her fin-

gertips across his forehead. "As sweet as I think your gesture is, you don't have to save me."

A pleasant warmth settled over him at her touch, leaving him oddly disoriented. "Yes, I do."

She dropped her hand to her side. "I don't mind what others say about me. You and I, *we,* know the truth."

Pete caught her hand in his, and turned it over in his palm. "I told Matilda Johnson we were getting married."

She snatched her hand free. "You…you… *what?*"

He spoke more slowly this time. "I told her we were getting married."

She did *not* like his answer. That much was made clear by her scowl. "You shouldn't have done that."

"She was blaming you for luring me into my own storm cellar."

The color leached out of Rebecca's cheeks as she sank into a nearby chair. "I…I simply don't know what to say."

"Say yes. Mrs. Johnson is a bully. Our marriage will silence her. I'll speak with the pastor today and—"

"No."

"—schedule the ceremony at once." His words came to a halt. "What did you say?"

"I said, no." She rose cautiously, her palms flat on her thighs as though to brace herself. "I won't marry you."

"You're turning me down? After everything that's happened today?"

"No. I mean, *yes*. I'm turning you down."

"Your reputation—"

"Is my concern, not yours."

She sniffed, rather loudly, but she didn't give in to her emotions. Oh, she blinked. And blinked. And *blinked*. But no tears spilled from her eyes.

Pete pulled in a hard breath. He'd never been more baffled by a woman. "We were both in my storm cellar," he reminded her through a painfully tight jaw. "That means we share the burden of the consequences equally."

Blink, blink, blink. "My decision is final."

"So is mine. We'll be married by the end of the day."

Her breathing quickened to short, hard pants. And then…*at last*…it happened. One lone tear slipped from her eye.

"Rebecca, please," he whispered, knowing his soft manner came too late.

"No." She wrapped her dignity around her

like a coat of iron-clad armor. "We have nothing more to say to each other."

Just as another tear plopped onto the toe of her shoe, she turned and rushed out of the kitchen.

Stunned, Pete stared at the empty space she'd occupied. "That," he said to himself, "could have gone better."

* * * * *

Will Pete be able to change Rebecca's mind and salvage her reputation? Find out in HEARTLAND WEDDING, available in February 2010 only from Love Inspired Historical.

Love Inspired®

SUSPENSE

RIVETING INSPIRATIONAL ROMANCE

Watch for our new series of
edge-of-your-seat suspense novels.
These contemporary tales
of intrigue and romance
feature Christian characters
facing challenges to their faith...
and their lives!

NOW AVAILABLE IN REGULAR & LARGER-PRINT FORMATS

Steeple
Hill®

Visit:
www.SteepleHill.com